The Cave of Darkness
Book Two in The Transporter Series

Rachel Lopez

rachelrlopez.com

For information contact:
Synecdoche Publishing
synecdochepublishing.wordpress.com

Edited by Emily Burkey and Amanda Hovseth
Book design by Amanda Hovseth
Cover by Magpie Designs, Ltd, 2018
Images courtesy of Pixabay

ISBN: 978-1-945018-14-5 (soft cover); 978-1-945018-15-2 (eBook)

Library of Congress Control Number: 9781945018145

First Edition: 2018

DEDICATION

To my children…without you I would never have experienced the joyful love that God gifts to those who are blessed enough to be called mother.

To my street team you all ROCK! Jill, Mary, Robin, Stacy, Missy, Gregory, Reanna, Karline, Rhonda, Sandy, Amy, Heidi, Maryjane, Angela, Julie, Marla, and Adriana

And to my parents, thank you for putting up with me all those years when I was a wild teen and even now as a wacky adult.

I love you all!

CONTENTS

Chapter One

The Geek's Lair

From the outside, 1200 Pinewood Lane appeared to be a successful logging company. In a manner of speaking, a logging operation actually was being run from the quaint building. One of the Geeks—a group of scientists who once worked for my evil demon grandfather—had a fixation for chopping down trees. He was a logger by day and a scientist by night. I couldn't help but grin at the unlikely mix—scientists and lumberjacks.

"Cass, you weren't kidding about the Geeks' lair," I said, stepping around my tall curvy friend to get a better view. "Wright's Logging Company" was an effective ruse. The building—a modern A-frame cabin with tinted windows—lumbered before us.

Cassy's eyes scanned the property, making sure we were alone. Then she strolled to the building and pulled back a metal 'no-smoking' sign affixed to the side of the structure. Behind the sign was a keypad.

Shielding the keypad with her body, Cassy punched in a code. Seconds later a click resounded, and the glass doors swung open. Bubba ushered me inside and pulled me across the lobby by my elbow. Cassy was quick on our heels.

The main foyer was sparse yet modernly decorated. To my right a set of French doors opened to a meeting room. In the middle of the room a beautifully finished slab of wood sat upon a pedestal surrounded by rich, mahogany leather chairs.

A circular receptionist desk filled a majority of the entryway. The desk was littered with plans for elaborately crafted wooden furniture. I held back to closely examine the sketches.

Having released my arm, Bubba continued ahead, unaware I had slowed my pace. However, Cassy was quick to urge me on by applying firm pressure to my lower back with the palm of her hand. She guided me to the back of the room where a lit-up antique soda machine flickered and hummed.

Bubba pressed the orange soda button with his knuckles and instantly a hidden panel slid open, revealing a tiny elevator. As soon as the doors swung open Cassy pushed me inside. She and Bubba quickly swept the room with their eyes before the doors enclosed us in the tiny cart.

Who are these people? Secret service? I mused to myself.

The elevator was just big enough to accommodate Cassy, Bubba, and myself, quite uncomfortably. Wedged between Cassy's slim figure and Bubba's gigantic football player frame, I squeezed my shoulders inward, causing my already tense muscles to knot up. Looking from Cassy to Bubba, I tried to piece together all the information I had unearthed over the last twenty-four hours.

I desperately wanted to ask my only two friends how they could have hidden their identity all these years, but I wasn't ready for a confrontation. My mind was on overdrive, and I needed time to decompress before accosting anyone.

Instead, I turned my focus to the fact that Cassy's normally olive skin appeared greenish under the harsh fluorescent lighting of the elevator. Even with green-tinted skin Cassy was incredibly beautiful, her precisely cut hair shrouded her face like a sheet of fine black silk. The lighting did nothing to Bubba as he stood with the same wide grin which almost always covered his sun-kissed face.

Cassy reached across me and pushed the emergency switch on the elevator panel. I cupped my hands over my ears—no alarm sounded. Instead the elevator cart lurched downward. Cassy, Bubba, and I stood in deafening silence as we moved deep below the earth's surface.

For several minutes the tiny cart moved downward. I wrapped my sweat-soaked hands around the handrail so tightly my knuckles turned white and my ears popped. Before I could open my mouth to complain, a light ding rang throughout the elevator indicating we had arrived at our destination.

Once again Cassy reached over me and pushed a series of buttons. As the doors slid open, I gulped a large amount of air and almost choked on it. Apprehension gripped me. This place would soon become my home and there was little I could do to change that fact, as much as I might want to.

Cassy and Bubba simultaneously stepped out before me, momentarily blocking my view. When they moved aside–allowing me a glance into the room–my jaw dropped.

Chapter Two

Glass and Chrome

The Geeks' compound was a scientist's dream with its state-of-the-art—everything. The well-polished surfaces reflected tiny balls of blinding light into my eyes. Bright lighting gave the illusion that the laboratory was above ground which lessened the impending claustrophobia that inevitably came from living underground. Or at least that is what Cassy said on the drive over.

Once my eyes adjusted, I could make out several mini-laboratories leading off of the great room. My eyes explored every inch of the area I would now call home.

Before we reached the compound, Cassy had explained that the living quarters were nestled in the back of the compound, unseen from where we stood. I would have my own mini-apartment which I imagined would feel odd. With exception to a few overnight cheer trips, I'd never been on my own before. The compound also housed a cafeteria, gym, and library, along with a great many laboratories.

Cassy's description of the compound didn't do the place justice, and I wasn't ready for the scene I walked into. Each door was a glossy black metal with a rectangular piece of glass in the center. The dark doors stood out against the rest of the environment as every other surface was draped in chrome and white.

Pungent antiseptic cleaner filled my nostrils, and a twinge of panic hit my stomach, but I stopped it in its tracks. Later I would afford myself time to feel the brunt of what I was experiencing, but now wasn't the time.

A couple of laboratory doors hung open. Inside the rooms, state-of-the-art microscopes and equipment perched upon stainless steel tables and countertops. Having such an elaborate outfit eliminated the need for the Geeks to leave the compound.

Before my mishap with my mom trying to kill me and a few accidental trips to Hell, Cassy, Bubba, and their families were able to come and go as they pleased. Now, however, we had to be careful about going in and out so as not to raise suspicion. The Geeks were being watched. There was serious doubt anyone would be able to leave the compound for a long time, and now more than ever we were all in grave danger.

"Meadow, darling," Mrs. Romano, Cassy's mother, wrapped me in her arms.

My throat seized at her touch. Closing my eyes, I melted into her embrace. The realization of never again being able to receive comfort from my own mother hit me in the gut.

"Mrs. Romano," I said squeezing her tightly; allowing her flowery scent to invade my nose. Sensing my need to be held, she didn't let go.

To my horror, a sob broke free from my chest, then another, and another until I had no choice but to succumb to them.

"You poor darling, it's okay…it's okay. You're safe now," she consoled, her Italian accent as thick as honey. She patted my back and whispered words of reassurance until I calmed down.

When I finally pulled away, I noticed an audience had surrounded us. The awkward group at least had the decency to look away and act as if they hadn't witnessed my breakdown. Of course, Cassy and Bubba were still there. Bubba's parents, the Parkers, Cassy's parents, the Romanos, a couple of men I didn't know, and a woman who looked slightly familiar all stood in a semicircle around me. They were dressed in black uniforms resembling wetsuits, paired with black combat boots. A few of the men wore lab coats over their suits.

I stood in my cheer uniform from the night before, feeling childish and uncomfortable. It was that or a backless hospital gown—a reminder of my mother's betrayal. At the moment, cheerleading and high school seemed light years away. I should have been at home studying for finals and preparing for graduation, but that life was over. After all that had happened,

I could never go back.

In truth, there was nothing to go back to. My mother and father had fled after my mother attempted to end my life. Likely they had joined the rest of the Ganders who were on the hunt for me and my friends in hopes of finishing their crude experiments. Even Mark was gone, stuck in Hell, waiting for me to rescue him from Satan and his fiends.

"Hi," I waved awkwardly to the group at large, looking down at my scuffed-up cheer shoes.

One of the men broke from the group and walked over to me, placing his hands on my shoulders. He stood silently until I looked up at him. The man appeared to be around my father's age; however, where my father was short and stocky, this man was tall, slender, and had a receding hairline. The intense lighting reflected off his thick lenses, concealing his eyes.

"It's good to see you again, Meadow. I haven't laid eyes on you since you were a baby. I don't suppose you remember me." He had the face of a man who had never laughed a day in his life—and he was correct. I didn't remember him. "I was friends with your parents when we worked at Ganders. My name is Dr. James Wright."

"A pleasure to meet you, Dr. Wright," I said softly. I took a step back, breaking the hold he had on my shoulders, and extended my hand to him. A pained look crossed his face as he firmly gripped my hand in his.

He bowed his head slowly then walked back to the group. The next person to introduce himself was a short, stout, middle-aged Asian man with light green eyes, a warm smile, and a head full of the shiniest black and silver hair I had ever seen. Unlike Dr. Wright, this man's eyes were framed by smile lines—the sort of person I could share a good laugh with.

"Meadow, I'm Dr. Will Ross." His eyes crinkled around the edges, putting me at ease. "I started studying transporters a few years back when I met my wife, Beth." He pointed behind him with his thumb, but I kept my eyes fixed on him. "I suppose you would consider me the newbie of the group. Beth shared with me all she knew about the Ganders and I've been working with these guys here to gain knowledge to keep you safe." I nodded my head at the man, instantly liking his gentle demeanor.

"Thank you," I said, not sure what to say. It was strange hearing there were people out there protecting me when I hadn't even known I needed protection.

"This is my wife, Beth." He gestured for a second time to the woman behind him. This time my eyes shifted to hers. His wife, a few inches taller than me, donned blondish hair and a shy smile. She favored my mother slightly and my heart broke, realizing once again what I had lost. The woman's arm was in a sling and she clenched her jaw as she stepped forward.

My eyes widened in surprise when I recognized her. "Oh...you're...you're okay!" The young woman who stood before me was the same lady my mother had shot the night before. Beth had tried to protect me, and she'd almost been killed in the process.

"Oh this?" She pointed to her injured arm and shook her head. "I'll live. I have some healing to do but I'll be fine. Besides, I have a wonderful doctor." Beth shared a loving glance at Dr. Ross who smiled back at his wife and then ducked his head shyly.

"Thank you...for saving me," I said and shook her uninjured hand. She winced slightly–clearly in more pain than she let on.

"No biggie. Once I found out what the Ganders were up to, I had to do something. Even though they closed the lab and abandoned the building, I knew they were far from done. I continued to research and study as much as I could, then I met my husband. Shortly afterward we teamed up with these guys and started to search for the Ganders. We had no luck, until Ray contacted me..."

"Ray?" Ray is the name of my grandfather who resides in Hell. *Could it be the same Ray?*

"Yes, he was taken to Hell shortly after the Ganders fell, but from time to time he likes to contact me...uh...telepathically." She shifted uncomfortably. "Ray and I had a unique relationship when I worked at Ganders."

"A relationship?" I made a face and my entire body cringed.

Beth laughed but composed herself quickly. "Um, not that kind of relationship. Ray is my father. He didn't know I existed until I was nineteen, when my mother passed away. She left me a note explaining who my real father was and where to find him if I chose to. Ray wasn't a great guy back when he and my mother...um...when they met. He still isn't, to be frank." Beth sighed.

"Why would you seek him out if he was so bad?" I asked.

"Because he's my father and I thought maybe he had changed. Eighteen years is a long time for someone to change their ways. Plus, I was alone. Sometimes bad company beats none at all," she answered simply then continued her story. "Shortly after we met, Ray hired me to work as an assistant to the scientists at Ganders, so we could get acquainted. However, he asked that I hide the nature of our relationship from everyone. He didn't want to hurt his wife and daughter." *His daughter–she means my mother!*

"That must have been..." I searched for the right words, *lonely* came to mind.

"I was willing to do anything I could to have family in my life, even if it meant hiding my identity. It was tough watching Ray with Nancy. He loved her, I could tell. I stayed in the shadows following the scientists around whenever they would let me. I was a bit nosey in my younger years. It was during that time that I found out about the transporter experiment."

"Wait! So you're like...my aunt?!" I asked.

"Um I...I suppose so...yes. I never thought of...I mean you're adop—" Her words stopped short, the red in her face quickly replaced by a sickly white.

"Adopted? Yes, I heard what my mother said in the Gander building." Despite myself my jaw trembled. Another crying fit was in my near future. "I hoped it wasn't true but..." But it was and there was nothing I could do about it; I wasn't ready to tackle that notion yet.

"I'm sorry." Beth watched me closely. She—like her husband—was a kind soul.

"After all I have learned in the past twenty-four hours, being adopted is the most *normal* thing that has happened to me. However, I am confused about how I am able to communicate with Ray telepathically when we aren't related by blood?"

"What do you mean?" Dr. Ross asked, his eyes lighting up in fascination. Dr. Wright also perked up, taking a step closer to hear what I had to say.

"He communicates with me as well, or he did before I left the hospital. He came to me in my mind. It was foggy, and I could just barely see his face. He said Mark needed my help...that I should go to Ganders and look in room 300. There is something in his desk." I scrunched up my face, trying to remember exactly what Ray had said. Our conversation felt like it had been weeks ago.

"There's no way we can go now. That place will be crawling with Ganders," Dr. Wright said drily. I opened my mouth to argue but all the air was squeezed from my lungs as a strong set of arms encircled me from behind.

"Meadow! Thank God!" A muscular being swung me in the air. My body tensed. I didn't need to see him to know who he was—the feel of his arms around me...the scent of warm spice that invaded my nostrils.

"Back off, bucko," Cassy said wedging herself in between me and...*Evan*. Evan Jacobs—my ex-boyfriend who I had loved dearly once upon a time. He loosened his grip and put me down but didn't let go. My body went stiff and I didn't dare move.

Cassy put her arm around my shoulder and leaned into Evan's personal space, giving him the death stare. "You have no right to talk to her after all she's been through. This compound is big enough that you can steer clear of her. Consider this your only warning." Cassy was fuming mad as she mashed her long, perfectly-manicured nails into Evan's chest, nearly pulling my head off in the process.

Evan stepped closer to Cassy, dragging me with him, ready to share his feelings on the subject but Bubba intervened. He slapped his hand firmly on Evan's shoulder, steering him away from us, forcing Evan to finally let me go.

"Let's cool off, man. We asked you not to come around tonight." Bubba looked my way apologetically, his normal grin replaced with a scowl. I didn't realize I had been holding my breath during the exchange but the moment Evan released me, all the air in my lungs whooshed out at once. Feeling lightheaded, I leaned against Cass.

One of the many advantages to having Bubba as a friend was his size. There weren't many people who would challenge his six foot, two hundred fifty-pound frame, not even Evan who was mighty full of himself. Evan knew Bubba had a heart of gold but also that he wouldn't allow anyone to hurt the people he loved, especially when Cassy was involved. Not to mention, Bubba had a way with Evan no one else did.

Evan backed away, but before he had taken five steps he turned to me and said, "I'm sorry." I wasn't sure if he meant about the striking blonde I had caught him with in his college dorm or the situation I now faced. Either way a curt nod was all he received in response. I watched him walk away with my arms pressed firmly to my side, praying no one but Cassy could see my body tremble.

"What was that about?" I asked once Evan was out of earshot. Craning my neck around I shot an accusatory look at the group at large.

Dr. Wright cleared his throat loudly before he spoke. "Well, the Jacobs family was once a part of Ganders as well but after the split occurred they wanted out indefinitely. We saw no reason to force them to stay; however, we monitor them to make sure they don't join the...the other side."

The other side...the dark side... I concealed a snicker. The last twenty-four hours had taken its toll on my ability to react with appropriate emotions. I was moments from breaking into a crying-laughing fit of hysterics. "They ensured your protection while you and Evan were together," the doctor continued.

My head snapped back as the realization of what the doctor said took shape in my brain. I hoped the conclusion I was jumping to wasn't true. Everyone in the room but Dr. Wright looked away, fixing their eyes on different points of the room. "In what way?" I asked cautiously.

Dr. Wright paused before he spoke. "Not all of us were convinced your parents fled Ganders to start a better life. To keep you safe I approached the Jacobses and convinced them to persuade Evan to court you, once you were of proper dating age, of course. It was perfect. You kids all grew up together so it made sense to put the two of you together. Once Evan gained your trust he was able to watch over—"

"Wow...wait....what are you saying now?" My voice a dull rumble. It was true then. No wonder Evan seemed so cold when I spoke of joining him at college. It was when he could be free to live his life. Free of me and the burden he carried having to babysit someone he didn't care for.

A rush of blood flowed through my body, invading my ears, and I could only hear every other word Dr. Wright spoke. "I'm sorry...but it was...the only choice we had."

"I'm sure it was, Dr. Wright. The. Only. Choice!" I spoke through clenched teeth.

The level of betrayal was too much to bear. My heart crumbled inside my chest. "How can you people play with another person's life? Haven't I suffered enough?" My voice shook; my lips trembled. I looked at each of them one by one—people I had known my entire life with the exception of a select few. They had all known, yet they let me fall in love with a boy who was forced to be with me. It made sense why he messed around at college; he had never loved me to begin with.

Lies.

Betrayal.

Bitterness reached its boiling point and threatened to spill over. My chest heaved, the room spun, and the whooshing in my ears was deafening.

"I'm sorry you're hurt, but I'm not sorry for doing what I did. You're too valuable to the cause." Dr. Wright's robotic mannerism sounded anything but sorry. I instantly disliked him—and, at that moment, most of the occupants of the room.

"And what cause would that be?" I snapped. Dr. Wright had made the list of people I wanted to throat punch, but I wouldn't because I was a good Christian girl and it wasn't the right thing to do. *Maybe if I asked for forgiveness afterwards…*

Dr. Wright opened his mouth to answer. "James, now isn't the time." Hugo Romano stepped between us. "She has been through enough and needs rest. I know it's difficult for you to do, but stop being a scientist and act like a caring human being for a few minutes." He gestured for his wife to take me away.

"My apologies," Dr. Wright mumbled, his voice lacking sincerity.

"Come, Meadow," Mrs. Romano said, gently tugging at my arm. I resisted for a moment, shooting a venomous look at the room full of traitors. Finally, I gave in and followed her. I needed time to think, to process, to cry.

Once out of earshot Mrs. Romano apologized. "Sorry about James. He means well. He just doesn't understand human emotion unless it pertains to milling wood or a scientific breakthrough."

"Where are we going?" I asked numbly.

"To your living quarters. Cass said she briefed you on the compound but tomorrow you will get a full tour of the complex. This is your home for now and you should feel free to go and explore where you like. All we ask is that you respect the adults' living quarters and make yourself known before you barge in. Of course, I know that won't be a problem with you." She looked back at me, her large hazel eyes full of compassion.

"Why did you let this happen to me? I loved all of you like family." The words flowed from my lips before I could stop them, but I needed to know how they could have kept this from me.

"You have no idea how hard this was for all of us. Dr. Wright shouldn't have shared what he did this evening. There is so much more to this story, and no matter what happened between you and Evan—in the end we had to protect you. I know our secrecy hurts but we can't take it back." Her voice softened. "I think we all took for granted the power love has over youth."

I rolled my eyes. She had no idea the power I let Evan have over me. "Why is Evan here? Dr. Wright said the Jacobs wanted out." I was afraid to say more in case my tongue lost the ability to be tamed.

"Evan joined us…Geeks." The edges of her mouth turned up slightly. "I believe that is the term Cassy uses. He goes to school during the day and works as a lab assistant to Dr. Wright most evenings. He has sacrificed a lot to be here to support you."

"How kind of him," I grumbled under my breath, thinking about how he didn't give up too much of his social life while he was at college.

"Don't be too hard on him, Meadow. Evan tried, he just…he should explain himself to you one day. But for now, we will do our best to keep him away, and you will be so busy it isn't likely you two will run into one another." Mrs. Romano's mouth formed into a tight grimace. "He was warned not to disturb you tonight but apparently he will need a reminder on following orders if he plans to remain here with us. I will do all I can to keep an episode like tonight from happening while you're here in the compound."

"What will I be doing?" I asked.

"Cassy tells me there is a young man who needs your help, correct?"

"Mark." I nodded.

"The only way to save him is to sharpen your skills and learn some new ones. Fortunately for us, your mom actually did something useful and put you in martial arts for all those years. However, you will have to learn a new skill set that will make you deadly. I don't know how you survived being in Hell for so long without proper training, but we cannot take any chances moving forward. You could have been slain down there." Mrs. Romano's choice of words caused a tremor to run through my body.

We had traveled for quite some time and were approaching an area where sliding glass doors lined each side of the walkway. In front of some of the doors were welcome mats and large potted plants that appeared almost real. *But surely*, I thought, *real plants wouldn't survive without the sun's rays.*

Mrs. Romano continued on as I admired each doorway, some of them decorated with the same stringed lights that could be seen on one's back porch during a summer barbecue—flamingos, tiki heads, and pineapples.

"Starting tomorrow you will be trained in hand-to-hand combat, along with training to enhance your transporting skills. Since you have the gift of telepathy, we would like you to practice that as well. I do wonder, however, how you can communicate with Ray, not being his blood relative. We assumed Beth shared that gift with him because of their bloodline."

I began to wonder how much further we had to go when Mrs. Romano stopped and guided me through another set of sliding glass doors.

"Here is where you will be staying when you have free time. It's all yours. Hugo, Cassy, and I are just a few doors down that way at the bend." She pointed, but I was too busy taking in my new home.

My suite was impressive—the apartment incredibly modern. I suddenly felt grown up. To the right a sitting room adorned with a large flat screen television, a white sofa, and a deep-blue sitting chair. To my left, a small kitchen equipped with the basics needed to survive: a mini-fridge, microwave, and dishwasher. I wondered how they furnished so many rooms unnoticed by anyone on the outside.

Mrs. Romano stood back quietly as I inspected the place. Just past the dining area was my bedroom. I wandered to the place where I would lay my head. Cassy must have had a hand in decorating the room for me as there were posters of my favorite movies and musicians hung on the walls. Draped across the plush bed was a fuzzy lavender bedspread, a few shades lighter than the violet paint on the walls. Off to the side of my bedroom was a tiny bathroom.

To my disappointment there was a standing shower but no bathtub. The bathroom was decorated...interestingly...with rubber duckies plastered everywhere—the shower curtain, bath mat, even the toothbrush holder was covered in tiny yellow ducks. I chuckled. The rubber duckies weren't what I would have chosen for myself, but Cassy knew I would find them amusing.

She was right. An unexpected pang of jealousy hit me in the gut. She knew me so intimately and I knew so little about who she really was. She knew when I was a little girl I bathed with dozens of rubber duckies each night. I was ten before I gave them up and only because Cass and Evan teased me about them. Bubba tried to defend me back then, but eventually he concluded I should let them go as well.

Lying on the bathroom counter was a set of nightclothes. "You need to get ready for bed, sweetheart. You have a long day tomorrow; the doctors are eager to start your training."

"Yes ma'am," I said, suddenly afraid to be alone.

"If you feel you're being pushed too hard, come to me."

I nodded. "Will Cassy and Bubba train with me?" Although I was still very much angry with them, there was comfort in knowing they would be close by.

"Cassy and Bubba have been training their entire life," Mrs. Romano explained softly, sensing my distress. "You need our attention now. I'm afraid Cassy and Bubba have limitations and will be of no help to you."

"I need all the help I can get. The only reason I made it through my trips to Hell so far is sheer luck."

"Believe me when I say one day you will realize your full potential. Although, I wish none of you children had to endure what you're going through." Mrs. Romano's eyes reflected guilt.

"So, Cassy and Bubba won't be able to help me?" I asked again.

Mrs. Romano shook her head sadly. "Cassy and Bubba have only been able to transport a few times to the Caves of Hell, their souls can't handle the extreme change from the earth plane. They have no choice but to come back immediately."

"What's the point of this? Why do the Geeks want me? I can almost see why the Ganders do but...what's my purpose here?"

"We only want what's best for you, to give you the tools necessary to handle the life you have been given. Get some rest now. You will be needing it in the days to come. Goodnight, sweet girl." Mrs. Romano gave me a hug before she left.

"Good night, Mrs. Romano." I said softly.

After she left, I turned on the shower as hot as I could stand it, hoping I might be able to wash off this terrible day and all the betrayals I'd faced over the last several hours.

*　　　　*　　　　*

That night sleep was hard to come by. I tossed and turned. Out of desperation I called out to Ray in my mind. This time I could only hear him, not see him.

"Child, what are you doing?" Ray asked gruffly.

"Why can't I see you?"

"It takes too much of my strength to do that very often."

"Oh," I said. "I'm in hiding now."

"Doing what exactly?"

"Preparing for a fight," I replied feebly.

He growled. "You won't win."

"Then I will die trying. I have nothing to lose." I was trying my best to keep it together. I wasn't ready for another fight. I was ready to hide under my blankets for the rest of my life if necessary.

"Ha, save your bravery for someone who believes it," he taunted.

"One day the pits of Hell will be cleared of the innocent souls Satan has trapped down there." My own words reminded me that my curse could have a deeper purpose. There were people suffering, maybe I could help them.

"Ah, I see…well, your first task will be near impossible. Your boyfriend is stuck in the Cave of Darkness and there's no way you will find him." Ray cackled. I didn't get the man. It was like part of him cared and part of him was pure evil.

"How are we able to communicate with one another? Beth thought it was because you're her father, but I'm not your blood, am I?" I asked, half hoping and half scared that he may in fact be related to me somehow.

Ray became quiet for a moment and when he spoke I could almost hear a smile in his voice. "I didn't know she claimed me as kin. No, you aren't a blood relative of mine, but you are still family. All the transporters came from orphanages across the world."

I wanted to ask where I was really from, but we needed to stay on track. "I don't know much about who or what she claims. How am I able to communicate with you then?"

"It's not about being blood related. The Dark One bestows his loyal followers with gifts. I chose to communicate with…" he paused for several seconds "…with those on the other side who would be beneficial to converse with."

"Why would I be beneficial to communicate with? And why now? Why have you never reached out to me before?"

"Your parents would have locked you up had you told them you were talking to me when they know good and well I am dead."

"True, mom took me in to see Dr. Barnes anytime I got too angsty."

"Not surprising…you may also like to know you can communicate with anyone that I can telepathically. That gift may come in handy for you one day soon."

So, I can talk to Ray and *Beth.*

"Is there anyone else I can converse with?"

"None that would benefit you." Ray sounded bored.

"How do I save Mark?"

"Figure it out on your own. I allow myself to get involved only when I deem it necessary. Mark isn't my problem and he won't be yours soon."

"What does that mean?" I asked, no longer trying to hide my aggravation.

"In a matter of days Mark will give in to the Dark One. No one can last in the Cave of Darkness for long." Ray's laugh grated on my nerves.

"How long?" I asked.

"A week, two at the most, and that's if he is strong enough to fight his own demons." Ray dismissed my concern. "Did you make it to Ganders yet?" Talking to him was like talking to a child bouncing from one subject to another.

"No, they say the place is heavily guarded," I answered distractedly.

"I suppose it would be by now," Ray huffed. "Oh well, you aren't ready for its power yet anyway." Seeming offended for some reason unbeknownst to me, his presence left my mind.

"Ready for what power? Ray?" He really was gone. "READY FOR WHAT?" I shouted in my mind, but he didn't answer. All I received was deafening silence.

*   *   *

It felt as if I had just fallen asleep when Cassy woke me. "Wakie, wakie," she sang, flipping the lights on. I groaned, ready to have her head. From the moment her eyes opened each morning Cassy was all rainbows and butterflies—in my opinion the single most annoying trait one could have.

"Go away, I didn't sleep well." I rolled over on my side pulling the

16

blanket over my head.

"Well, I feel for you then because the Geeks have major plans for you today and they will accept no excuses to miss training. Believe me, I know."

I could almost hear her face scrunch into a scowl. All those times Cassy had to bail on plans and disappeared during school breaks made sense now. "They're annoying like that. Now get up sleepyhead." Cassy shifted back to joyful annoyance while pouncing on the side of my bed like a pup waking its master.

"Ugh, why, why, why?" I yelled into my pillow, slamming my fists into the bed on either side of my head. *Could I not have one stinking day? My mom had tried to kill me just a few hours ago.*

"Aren't you ready to save that super cutie from the fiery pits of Hell? It will make for the start of a smoking hot relationship," Cassy kidded. Her sense of humor was slightly more twisted than mine.

"Lord help your soul, Cassy Romano, if you don't get out of here in the next five seconds. Now, get out!" I tossed my pillow at her head, missing by a foot.

She skipped to my door. "You have ten minutes. Oh, and wear your training gear. It's hanging in your closet." I tossed another pillow. It too missed and bounced off the wall.

Stumbling over to my closet, I asked God to give me strength for whatever I had gotten myself into. My eyes bugged out of my head when I opened the doors to my closet and saw ten identical black outfits, the same outfits the Geeks wore the night before, hanging neatly in a row.

There was very little clothing besides the somber garb. I gulped, realizing the uniforms were meant to be form fitting. My body wasn't made for all that. Irritated, I grabbed one of the garments and headed to the shower.

Cassy stuck her head in my bedroom door just as I finished up. "You ready?"

"Yeah, admiring my new wardrobe," I called back sarcastically, looking at myself in the full-length mirror affixed to the bathroom door.

The bottoms were saggy, bringing attention to my lack of a derriere, and the top was so tight I looked like a flat board with a head attached. My feet were weighed down with thick ugly black commando boots. The only comfort I had was my socks (another gift from Cassy) sporting cartoonish green frogs with large red lips saying *You are Toad-ally Awesome.*

"Well, at least they match everything," she said checking me out. "Come on, I'm starving." Cassy must have gone back to her room to change while I showered because she now donned the same outfit as me; however, she looked like she was ready to play the sultry spy from a James Bond movie. I rolled my eyes. *Of course, she did.*

Before we walked out of the room I twisted my mane of hair into a tight bun and gave myself one last look. My eyes were empty and encircled by dark gray bags. The innocent cheer queen was gone. Now all that remained was the shell of a girl haunted with pain created by those she loved.

"Let's go." I turned on my heels, determined not to think of who I used to be but instead focus on the person I had to become in order to save Mark.

Side by side, Cassy and I walked towards the main laboratory, the thick rubber soles of our boots squeaking with each step we took. Once we reached the main corridor, I could see all the doctors standing in a line ready to greet us. To my pleasure Evan wasn't among them. As I approached the group, they broke out in applause. It caught me off guard, but I continued towards them, trying not to smile at the absurdity of the situation.

Dr. Wright stepped out of the line and intercepted me. "Are you ready?"

With a firm nod of my head I eloquently answered, "Yeah, let's rock."

Chapter Three

Marcus: The Swinging Tree 1891

The night air grew cool–it felt nice against his skin. A light fog slowly wound itself through the rows of unharvested corn. He looked up at the millions of tiny stars in the clear night sky. His sister was right. He had taken the beauties of the world for granted. Now it was too late to appreciate it. These were his last moments.

Marcus ambled through the fields he loved, recalling the countless hours spent working the soil he stood on. He took in the scent of the earth and let it fill him, wondering if the pain would last long or if his life would simply snuff out. Marcus tilted his head and narrowed his eyes on something up ahead. The swinging tree.

The swinging tree—a twisted aged oak—stood proudly alone to the left of the cornfields. Should that be where his life would end? It had been his favorite place as a child. In his family Marcus typically received the short end of the stick when it came to toys and gifts. He was the next in line to become man of the family and that role started early on, meaning if Emma or Momma needed something, they got it before Marcus or his father— except for one special day.

On his sixth birthday his father had called for him to come outside. That was nothing new as his father had liked to take him around while he performed various duties, sharing with his son the importance of taking care of a farm. Marcus had enjoyed following his father around; he longed to be just like him when he grew up. So, when his father had handed him a few bundles of rope and a plank of wood, he had thought it was another lesson on farm upkeep.

"What are we fixin' today, Papa?" he had asked, turning his wide blue eyes to his father.

"Try to keep up," was his father's brisk reply. Marcus hadn't said another word. He was afraid if he asked any questions he would be sent back to Momma and Emma.

The two had walked in comfortable silence until they reached the oak tree the men used for shade while eating lunch during harvest time. His father had studied the tree, his eyes narrowing on a sturdy branch that jetted from the trunk. He had grabbed the bundles of rope from his son and heaved one end of each rope over the branch. "Hand me the board, son," his father had commanded.

Marcus had passed the plank to his father, perplexed as to what he was doing. He had watched intently as his father plunged the ropes through holes that had been bored into the wood on either end. His father had then tied knots at the end of each rope so they would suspend the wooden board into the air. Marcus had smiled when he had watched his father sit upon the plank then kick his legs out, swinging back and forth.

"Oh Father, you made a swing," Marcus had squealed with excitement but then the light in his eyes went out. "I'm sure Emma will love it, sir." His voice was hollow. After all, it was his twin's birthday as well and he understood boys on a farm didn't have time to play. They worked hard and took care of the women.

"Well yes, I'm sure Emma will love it, but son this is for you. This is your birthday gift and you can share it with Emma whenever you like, but this will be our special place to come and talk, to brush the worries of the day away, okay?"

Marcus had nodded, fervently trying to understand why tears poured from his eyes when he was so happy. "Yes, Papa!" *Our own special spot!*

"What are you waiting for? Try it out." His father had hopped up, gesturing for his son to give the swing a try. For over an hour Marcus had swung and laughed. It was his most treasured moment with his father. The two men had had many days like that over the years until one day it became a forgotten toy. Marcus had grown up.

The swing had long been abandoned but the board still hung from the tree. The once much-loved toy had been beaten by the seasons, stained green with algae. Marcus propped the shotgun he had taken from his father's room against the trunk of the tree. Carefully he sat upon the swing and gazed at the sky above, gently rocking back and forth, wondering how it had come to this.

He thought about the deal he'd made with the strange man in the field, knowing the man could be none other than the devil himself. He always believed in God and the devil but to meet one of those entities was more than his mind could bear.

"Our Gracious Heavenly Father, I have messed up. If You can hear me…if I'm not too far gone…please save my soul. Please forgive me for what I must do…to save Emma."

He waited for the skies to open, for the booming voice of God from above to give him the words of wisdom he sought. However, there was nothing but the melodic chirp of crickets singing their nightly lullaby. His hope faded.

Marcus hung his head and cried, wondering why God had forsaken him.

Chapter Four

Betrayal

"You have to eat," Bubba said, his face filled with concern.

"I'm just so exhausted." Even saying the words felt like a chore. "The Geeks had me in back-to-back training all day long." My head drooped dangerously close to my bowl of chili.

"You will do yourself and Mark no good if you don't take proper care of yourself. Carbs and protein are your friends." Of course, Bubba the athlete would worry about me taking the proper micro-nutrients into my body.

"You're acting like Cassy," I mumbled into my veggie sub.

"Sorry, what about Cassy?" Cass asked, sneaking up behind me. At the moment, it was only Cassy, Bubba, and me in the dining hall. The Geeks had come and gone thirty minutes before I made it down.

"Don't start. I'm tired and grumpy," I snapped.

"What else is new?" Cassy shot back with a glint in her eyes.

She had been trying to get a rise out of me for days. That was her way, to get me riled up and watch my temper spin out of control, but for the most part I had been stoic. Thoughts of Mark, Hell, and my parents filled my mind, creating a vortex of emotions I couldn't decipher. Shooting an evil glance her way, I continued to eat. Bubba was right. I needed food.

A few bites in and I began tearing into my food like a starved animal. My mannerisms must have been appalling as Cassy and Bubba both turned their gaze away from me while I devoured my food. Training had taken a lot out of me, and it truly had been a long day. The only thing more important than food was sleep. The quicker I ate, the faster I could hit my bed.

If physical training was going to be this difficult, I would need all the sleep I could get. Most of my life my father had pushed me in martial arts, and I did reasonably well in karate, but I had slacked off over the last few years to pursue cheerleading. Thankfully I was in decent physical shape or I would have never made it through the day.

Training was more brutal than anything I had dealt with; the Geeks were merciless. Dr. Ross—although still my favorite—was the worst. I was convinced he was some sort of secret assassin when in the training chamber—which was less a room and more a rocky chamber with dirt flooring and a sharp drop-off. The Geeks even installed heaters in the ground and ceiling in an effort to simulate what Hell felt like. It wasn't even close.

Dr. Ross became a different man. He was tough and full of vengeance, quick and cunning. I had a hard time keeping up. If I couldn't get the best of a man almost double my age, I was going to have a hard time fighting Satan's fiends.

My body grew more tired on earth than my soul did in Hell. I wondered if that meant our souls were in fact stronger than our fleshly shells? After an hour of training with Dr. Ross, my body would betray me, my legs shook like Jell-O, my instincts severely altered. He would throw punch after punch and kick after kick like a madman.

I dodged left, right, left, right—the moment I thought I had figured him out, he would pounce on me. If I met up with a fiend as wiry as Dr. Ross, my only hope would be to run for my life. Unfortunately, fiends are frighteningly fast.

Dr. Ross must have been thinking along the same lines because he had me work on maneuvers to temporarily disable my attackers. It was our best course of action since we were unsure if fiends could die—not to mention that the severe psychological effects of killing the beasts could cause harm to my soul.

"Better?" Cassy interrupted my thoughts.

Yes, I did feel a little better, but I didn't want to admit it to her. For the most part Cassy could read me better than I could. If I needed a laugh, she was there to give me a chuckle. If I was sad, she was my shoulder to cry on. That's how it had always been between us, but now my world had been turned upside down and I had no idea what I needed, and my mannerisms confused Cassy as well. I didn't know if she was truly my best friend, and I was too scared of the possible answer to ask.

"Sorry, I'm out of it. You know…new living arrangement, Mom, Dad, training…Mark…dodging Evan. It's a lot."

"I know." She reached across the table and patted my hand; I guess it was time for the sweet, sensitive Cass. "We're here for you, you know that, right?" she asked.

No, I didn't know. I slid my hand out from under hers and picked up my dinner tray. I looked hard at the girl I had grown up with. She and Bubba were two people which I had thought would always be there for me but now I wasn't so sure.

The Geeks, although kind, treated me like a science experiment. They were very different from the loving mother who raised me, the same woman who wanted me dead. Deception. Lies. My reality distorted.

My worst fear of being left alone had come to pass. Years of therapy and tons of meds to fight anxiety and separation issues but here was the truth. Here in an underground science complex I had been abandoned, stolen, and experimented on.

A mad laugh escaped between my lips as the harsh reality of my life hit me. Cassy and Bubba looked at one another in surprise.

Alone.

Cassy and Bubba were different. I didn't know who they were, and they would never understand me. It wasn't that they had changed in the way they treated me or even how they behaved, but it killed me to know they had this whole secret life I knew nothing about. The lack of information they shared, in fact, almost cost me my life.

As much as I wanted to throw my tray against the wall and yell until my lungs collapsed upon themselves, I didn't. "Yeah, sure. See ya in the morning," I excused myself. "Goodnight," I whispered quietly.

Cassy stood up to follow me, but Bubba grabbed her wrist and shook his head. The sweet, clueless boy we had grown to love showed a lot of insight in that moment.

In those first days of training, I abandoned my faith. Deep down I knew

I needed God, but I was beyond angry. My heart became overwhelmed with anger and hate for my situation, and sometimes for those around me. Fear of what Mark may be going through plagued every moment of my day.

Why did I deserve this life after my faithfulness to God? There were so many others who deserved to be punished. I didn't know what I thought should happen, all I know is I wanted to go back to my old life. But those thoughts were foolish–my old life was nothing more than smoke and mirrors.

It was about three days in when Cassy came to my room at bedtime. "Hey, can I come in?" She strolled into my bedroom and dropped beside me on my bed.

"Help yourself," I grumbled.

"I brought you these." She plopped down a brown paper sack filled to the brim with my favorite treats. "The Geeks said you haven't been eating well. It's Mom's week to cook and she is highly offended she hasn't seen you."

"Tell her I'm sorry. I just need time alone. My room is the only place I can get that time. Until now," I tacked on the last two words, distractedly peeking at the bag of snacks.

"Listen, I have no idea what you're going through, but I can see a change in you. And I don't like what I see." Cassy shook her head but locked her eyes on mine. "Don't build those walls up—not against the people who love you."

I rolled my eyes to keep tears from falling down my cheek. Did she not understand all I had been through? The ache in my stomach would never go away. It had been ingrained into my soul and whenever I thought it might lessen, it would hit me twice as hard. I was pushing myself mentally, the Geeks were pushing me physically, and Cassy was pushing me emotionally. There was no escape from my new reality. I literally couldn't go for a walk in fresh air. Being constantly stuck underground was suffocating.

When I opened my mouth to speak, my voice broke so I stopped and said nothing.

"Shhh, it's okay." Cass put her arm around my shoulders. "You don't have to talk to me now. I know life is crazy and I can't even imagine the pain you feel. But don't shut me out. I'm the same girl you always knew. I love you, you're my best friend, my sister. I'm here for you no matter what. Bubba is here for you no matter what. The Geeks...even if they seem...indifferent...they do care for you and what's best for you."

Pressing my lips together I remained silent. Through my anger I didn't understand how she could expect me to welcome her with open arms after knowing she hid so much from me. *Our. Entire. Life.*

We had been best friends since preschool. How could she keep such a secret from me? *How?* I mean she, Bubba, and the Romano family led two totally different lives, and they couldn't bother to let me in on this world I was so much a part of? I tried to stuff those negative feelings deep down but one day soon I was going to crack.

"Do you hear me?" She pulled back to look at me again.

I let the air flee my lungs loudly before answering. "Yeah, I'm tired, Cass. I need some rest. The Geeks have been hard on me. I have very little time before I transport to save Mark so there's *a lot* of pressure on me."

Cassy looked up at the ceiling and took in a deep breath. "You're right, I'm being selfish. I just want us to be okay, but you have bigger things on your mind right now. I get it. Goodnight, I will see you in the morning, at breakfast." She looked at me pointedly.

"Yeah, I'll be there. Thanks." I gave her a half smile before she left. Once she was gone I rolled over and pulled the blankets up over my shoulders.

My body ached. Every muscle in my body tightened into tense balls of pain. Not only were my muscles tense but my brain throbbed, ready to explode. The Geeks had developed a virtual simulation which replicated the three caves of Hell, or at least their perception of it. The simulation lacked a lot, and I was pretty sure they were way off the mark on everything.

During each simulation I spent most of my time in the dark while poorly constructed papier-mâché fiends were thrown in my path. Occasionally Dr. Ross would attack from behind and manage to knock the breath out of me. By day four we discontinued use of the simulation room completely and doubled up on hand-to-hand combat where the doctor continued to kick the stuffing out of me.

After dinner I would sit for hours talking to the Geeks about anything I could remember about the caves and what I had experienced. Our talks didn't amount to much as there was little I could tell them. My short list of what I did know included: 1) I needed to find whatever was in Ray's desk, 2) there was something called the Mezirot that the fiends thought was powerful or valuable, and 3) I was no more near getting either one of those objects than when I first started. An overwhelming feeling deep in my gut made me aware that both objects were vital to my rescue mission.

The objects became an obsession. Each night I tossed and turned in bed thinking about what they were, what they looked like, and what powers they held. The only comfort I felt was in knowing I had an idea where one of the items was. However, getting the object would be nearly impossible.

It was one of those nights in which said objects haunted my thoughts, and I got up to make myself a warm cup of tea when I saw the outline of a large figure pass by my door. The clock on my microwave read three a.m. No one should be moving about in the living quarters at that hour. There wasn't necessarily a curfew but by eleven p.m. we were asked not to roam the halls of the housing quarters out of respect for our peers.

I ran back to my room and nearly face planted when I stubbed my toe on one of my kitchen chairs. Hopping on one foot I made it to my bedroom and threw on my house shoes with large bunny heads attached to the front, complements of Cassy.

Silently I jogged down the hall following the retreating figure, my toe still throbbing, the bunny heads wobbling rapidly back and forth. It took a few minutes, but I caught up. There was no doubt that the figure was a man. He wore all black with a ball cap pulled far down on his head. He was almost to the elevator by the time I got close enough to figure out who he was—Mr. Romano. He stopped at the elevator door and instinctively turned towards me.

With nowhere to hide, I gave him a little finger wave while smiling sheepishly. Mr. Romano looked at me in my bunny slippers and red hair sticking up at all ends and gave me a confused smile. Bringing his index finger to his mouth, he shook his head and stepped backwards into the elevator, his lips pressed into a hard line in an effort not to laugh at my appearance. The doors closed quietly before him, taking him up to the lobby of Wright's Logging Company.

In the morning I would ask Cassy where her dad had been off to at that hour. We were all in danger now, and for any of us to be traveling out of the Geeks' lair without having backup was unwise.

I shuffled back to my quarters—the mysterious objects that had plagued my thoughts forgotten for the moment—and fell asleep for what felt like ten minutes before I was being shaken awake by a horror-stricken Cassy.

Chapter Five

Marcus: 1891

He should have pulled the trigger as soon as he made it to the swinging tree. The longer he waited, the harder his decision became. His soul was heavily burdened—he hated the pain he would undoubtedly cause his family.

The voice came back; he knew it would if he delayed. "Your life for hers," the voice hissed inside his head.

"Why does it have to be this way?" Marcus cried. "Can't I...can't I do something else?"

The voice didn't answer right away, then finally, "I need companionship, a son."

"I'm sorry?" Marcus asked, afraid he had misheard.

"You will do as I say or I will take your family as my own," the voice was a harsh whisper inside his head.

"Giv...give me more time. I promise before the sun comes up I will do as you ask." Marcus looked to his left and the man he met in the fields stood studying him curiously, his black eyes glistening in the light of the moon. Although no longer dressed in the shiny black threads from earlier, he was still dressed unusually in a blood red suit made of the same silky material the rich women at church wore.

"Why do you need a son?" Marcus asked. Confusion encompassed his fear. The man considered the question and walked closer to Marcus.

"I have many followers, those who serve me whether willingly or due to poor choices yet none of them care for me. Their loyalty derives from fear...from the love of my power."

"Why me? Why would I be any different?"

"Your loyalty to those you love surpasses any I have ever encountered. Even though it meant cutting your life short, you were willing to trade your life for your sister. Believe me when I say most people won't trade their lives for those they supposedly love. You live in a selfish world yet remain pure-hearted. Let's say I'm intrigued by you."

"Maybe people *are* selfish in the world." Marcus gestured around him. "But, mister, the people in *my* world are just not that way. They're kind and would give their lives for one another."

Satan pondered Marcus' words but grew bored with the conversation. He glared at Marcus, his eyes growing cold.

"Do as I ask, or your family will suffer a death like nothing your mind could comprehend. You have until sunrise."

The man vanished in a cloud of red smoke, leaving Marcus with no choice but to do as he was commanded.

Chapter Six

A Dark Cloud

"Cass, what's wrong?" I asked shooting out of bed. Mr. Romano's face came to my mind, something terrible must have befallen him.

"It's...it's dad. Oh God, Meadow..." Her sobs loud and violent jumped from her chest. "He was murdered, oh God...my dad." Her body heaved and shook. I stood paralyzed, my mind whirling.

The room spun, and the ground came out from under me–I dropped to my bed in hopes the world would stop spinning. The seriousness of our situation slapped me in the face. The reality of my new life had reared its ugly head, claiming one of our own.

"What happened?" I whispered, needing to know the answer and wanting to plug my fingers in my ears to prevent Cassy's words from penetrating my brain. Mr. Romano was like a second father to me. *How could he be gone?* He taught me how to make pasta from scratch and how to ride my bike without training wheels. He was just here—had I not watched him climb into the elevator not long ago?

"I don't know. Mom and the Geeks are talking right now but they won't let me in."

My temper flared.

"Oh, that's not happening!" Jumping to my feet, I threw my boots on without bothering to tie them and stomped off down the hallway in my cotton candy-covered pajamas and black clunky combat boots.

The mere thought of the adults keeping us out of the loop made my blood boil. They couldn't treat us like children if we were to fight the evils of Hell. We transporters had the right to know what was going on. Cassy, Bubba, and I were in as much danger as anyone else if not more so. We were being hunted like animals.

Cassy trailed behind me. "Meadow, what are you going to do?" I turned to my friend, her eyes red-rimmed. For once in her life she looked uncertain of herself and, even worse, scared.

"They won't shut us out!" I caught a glimpse of myself in the glass wall lining the dining hall. The chunky curls of my hair stuck out in a manner that would have made Medusa jealous, my face set in a scowl of anger which was the emotion I chose to overtake the despair that lingered below the surface.

"Cass," I said her name sharply. She was going into shock. I gently took her arm and guided her to the only laboratory with lights on. Bubba stood guard outside the room, his normally good-natured self replaced with a serious Bubba I hoped to never see again.

Mr. Romano was dead. It hit me. Gone. I circled my arm around Cassy's shoulder and squeezed tightly. Her sobs shook us both. Bubba took a few large strides towards us and encircled Cassy and me in a gentle embrace. We stood there for a long time. Cassy broke away first and looked intently at me, then to Bubba.

"Okay," she said, stiffening her back, looking more like my courageous friend, and brushed past us. She swung open the door to the laboratory— one of the few with an actual solid wood swinging door instead of sliding glass. I assumed they used it for added privacy.

"Wow, girls, wait." Beth stepped out of the room, holding her hands up to ward us off. She was no longer in her sling but she winced as she held her arms up.

Bubba stepped in front of her and sternly said, "Let them go." He left no room for argument. Beth's cheeks reddened at the thought of being told what to do by a high school kid, but she assented and allowed us to pass.

Cassy and I barged through the door at full steam. Mr. Romano's body lay limply across a steel table, the fluorescent lights illuminating his sickly pale body, etching the scene into my mind forever. I gagged and turned my head. I had a sudden urge to run back outside and angrily give Beth a piece of my mind for letting us through. They had yet to take the opportunity to close his eyes or set his mouth and I could still see the look of pain and horror on his bruised face. I covered my mouth to keep from crying out.

Memories flashed in my mind: Mr. Romano taking Cassy and I to the circus, then later at home pretending to be the ring master as Cassy and I went from wild untamed lions to delicate tightrope walkers. Saturday morning waffles for breakfast followed by long days in the park. They were my second family. Now my *only* family, and they were falling apart.

In my periphery, a flurry of movement caught my attention. Cassy's legs slid out from under her body and she fell to the ground. Mrs. Romano ran to her daughter, dropping to her knees, clinging to her only child.

The two women embraced, sobbing uncontrollably as their loved one lay dead before them. *Loved one. Mr. Romano. Hugo. Friend. Father. Gone. Dead.* In a trance I stood less than four feet away, watching helplessly as the people I loved suffered.

What can I do? What could I ever do? Our world was spinning out of control. *Control, I need control!* This was the moment; I had lost too much and was likely to lose more still. *I will take control.* The transporters would no longer answer to the Geeks.

I would make decisions for us now. The Geeks could stand with me or against me, whichever they chose, but I would call the shots.

"Dr. Wright," I said, speaking to the grief-stricken doctor with as much authority as I could muster, "what happened?"

The doctor looked at me blankly. "He broke into Gander's, looking for whatever it was Ray instructed you to find." Dr. Wright covered his mouth to stifle a sob. He closed his eyes. His words carried no accusation, yet I jerked back as if he had slapped me across the face. Mr. Romano died for me. Cassy lost her father, Mrs. Romano her husband—for me?

"Who killed him?" I asked, scanning the room. Dr. Ross and Evan stood off in a corner. No one answered.

Beth walked in with Bubba, each one of us took turns looking at the other. "Bubba, take Cassy and Mrs. Romano to my living quarters," I ordered. It was apparent no one else knew what to do. Bubba nodded and helped the women to their feet.

In my mind I said, "Beth, make them some tea, give them something to relax, and watch over them for me." Beth turned on her heels and followed. I was glad to know I could communicate with Beth telepathically. Thankful for the usefulness of Ray's gift I continued directing the rest of the crew who, at the moment, were too shell-shocked to make decisions.

"Now, I need all of you to listen to me," I said sharply to the rest of the people in the room, being careful not to look at Mr. Romano. "Mr. Romano is dead. *He. Is. Gone.* His death doesn't change our mission, I suggest we get ourselves together and move on. Training starts in one hour."

Every eye turned in my direction, and every mouth dropped open. Even I was surprised at how strong I sounded, because inside I was a wreck. Evan spoke from behind me. "Meadow is right. We must keep moving. We're running out of time and we must all work together."

"I'm glad you feel that way, Evan. You can prepare our breakfast and deliver it to conference room one," I called over my shoulder as I walked out of the room to check on Cassy and her mother.

Chapter Seven

A Fiend's Tale

"Okay, you're all set," Dr. Wright said, leaning over me. He lightly tugged on my EEG wires to make sure they were all firmly attached. "Meadow, you need to transport to the outer edge of the Water Cave. That seems to be easier for you. Clear your mind and visualize where you need to go."

"Got it," I said, relaxing on the cot provided for transporters. It would be a miracle if I could focus on anything after the events of the day. I was worried about Cassy and Mrs. Romano. The loss of Mr. Romano lingered heavily in the air.

"You know you could go be with the Romano family. This could wait," Dr. Wright suggested uncomfortably.

"No, I have to go, time is not on our side. Besides, there is nothing I could say or do to take their pain away. Believe me I know…" I trailed off thinking of my mother and what she had done. I wondered if it would hurt worse if she were dead? *No, her betrayal was worse than death.*

"Alright, let's get started then," Dr. Wright said stiffly with a slight shake of his head. I squinted my eyes at him. He was attempting to be kind but the stress of the last few days had nurtured a monster inside of me.

Even if I wanted to stay, today was the deadline the Geeks and I had set for my transport. It was the longest we felt comfortable leaving Mark in the Cave of Darkness. Any longer, and he might be lost to us forever if he wasn't already. I was not prepared to sacrifice another life today.

I was about to doze off when Beth burst into the room. "Dr. Wright, we need you to come see this quickly. It's..." Beth's eyes darted my way then she covered her mouth with her hand, finishing the conversation in a hushed whisper.

"Meadow, excuse me a moment...can you hold off on transporting, just a few moments." I opened my mouth to argue but the doctor was gone.

Fuming that they still felt the need to keep secrets, I used a few minutes to come up with a self-righteous speech on letting me and the other transporters be privy to all information. Then I allowed myself to lay back and think about Mark. Sweet, kind, naive Mark. He had been in my life for only a short period of time, yet his absence left me vulnerable. There was something about him—he understood me and what it was like to be different. Thinking of Mark and his sweet blue eyes, I drifted off.

A dampness coated the air that filled my lungs. "Crap," my voice bounced off the rocky cavern walls of the Water Cave. At least I transported where I needed to be, in the landing between the Water Cave and the Fire Cave.

How did I transport so quickly? Hopefully Dr. Wright would be back in the lab soon to monitor my body. Glancing around the cavern, I took a step forward to look around.

Without warning, my legs flew out from under my body. The pull of strong hands with sharp spindly nails wrapped around my ankles. Thankful for all my training, I ripped my legs from the clad iron grip and rolled from the fiend, jumping to my feet. I easily overtook the creature and put him in a headlock.

The vile thing was spitting mad, clawing and calling me names I could only assume were unfavorable. If I let the creature go, I would have a fight on my hands. There was only one thing I could do.

Within seconds of visualizing the laboratory room where my cot lay, I was back in the transport room with a fiend trapped by my side. Dr. Wright and Beth stood in the doorway of the lab, their faces frozen in astonishment.

In their defense, the whole scene had to look crazy. One moment I'm asleep on the cot and the next a red, scaly being appears gripped in my arms. The demon bucked like a wild bull and my hands slipped. The fiend broke loose from my embrace and bolted to the open door.

"Close it!" I wailed, snatching at the fiend, missing by inches. Dr.

Wright stared dumbly at the scene that unfolded. Luckily Beth had some sense about her and slammed the door shut before the monster could escape.

Frantically, I grabbed the first thing I could reach—a large glass bottle filled with an unknown clear substance—and smashed it over the fiend's head. The yellow lining of the monsters ugly black eyes faded. It sank to the ground, landing on its side. Beth, Dr. Wright, and I pounced on the vile creature, hoping it wouldn't wake until we could secure it.

Acrid fumes of ammonia filled the room, burning my eyes and throat. The vapor was too strong; we needed to move soon. "We need something to bind its arms and legs, quick!" Coughing, I scrambled to my feet, sliding on the broken glass.

I opened drawer after drawer, sifting through tongue depressors, gauze, and alcohol wipes. "Wait, check my lab coat pocket," Beth called to me, her voice strained. "I have some medical tape in there. It won't hold for long, but we have got to…get…out of here and get this guy into one of the holding chambers."

Frantically scanning the room, I spotted her jacket draped across a rolling chair. Digging in her pocket I found a tiny roll of tape, hopefully enough to tie down a freakishly strong demon. In less than a minute we had bound the monster by its hands and feet. Once the tape was securely wrapped around the monster's arms and legs to our satisfaction I opened the door to get fresh air. Out of all the bottles to smash over his head I had to pick ammonia.

"What…happened?" Dr. Wright asked through clenched teeth, his eyes wide in horror. He looked down at the unconscious monster, waiting for it to spring in attack.

"I transported," I explained sliding as close to the open door as possible. I sucked in as much of the sweet non-ammonia filled air as I could before I continued. "One minute I was on my cot, the next I was on the landing between the caves. This guy," I nudged the fiend with my boot, "was waiting for me. He was guarding a staircase leading down the gorge. I bet the Cave of Darkness is down there."

I don't know how I knew but there was a stirring deep inside my gut telling me Mark was down there. A bolt of terror ran through my body at the thought of what lay at the bottom of that chasm.

"It's likely," Dr. Wright said, wiping beads of sweat from his forehead with the sleeve of his lab coat.

"In past travels, I saw ledges with openings up and down the canyon," I explained. "Finding the right place will be difficult. Based on the fiend's reactions when the Cave of Darkness was mentioned, I'm sure it will be in the most isolated corner of the cave."

"How did you transport there and back so quickly?" Beth interrupted me.

"Well I... I have been exhausted. One minute I was thinking of Mark, then poof I was in the caves. I guess all our practice has paid off because I was able to return quickly," I said.

"Remarkable...I believe there is a deeper connection between you and this boy than meets the eye." A thoughtful look crossed Beth's face.

I shrugged and looked down at the fiend. "What do we do with this?" I asked, the ammonia beginning to invade my senses again.

"We have a chamber in the back," Dr. Wright suggested.

"What if he's one of those fiends who can transport?" I asked.

Dr. Wright sighed, running his hand over his balding head. "A long time ago a fiend latched onto Bubba when he came back from a trial transport. It was the last time Cassy or Bubba were allowed to transport. Bubba almost died in the struggle. We also realized that Cassy and Bubba's souls couldn't handle the change from one plane to another."

My mind went back a few years, remembering an automobile accident Bubba claimed he was in. He had odd bumps, bruises, and scratches all over his body. Back then I remember joking that he looked like he had been in a fight with a tiger. He and Cassy looked uncomfortable when I mentioned it—I realized now that he had probably been in a fight with a fiend.

I looked blankly at Dr. Wright, waiting for him to answer my question. "Uh, we ran tests on the fiend before it died, and we were able to come up with what we like to call the anti-transporter serum. The serum uses the fiend's own power to hold it here. It creates a barrier between the earth and Hell plane. The chamber the fiend will be kept in is double-paned; the space in between those panes are filled with the serum."

"Okay," I shrugged. "Let's move this guy before he wakes up." I groaned as I lifted the demon's bound feet. Dr. Wright lifted the beast by its hands, and together we half-carried, half-dragged the fiend from the transport room to a laboratory across the main corridor and down a long hallway that was rarely used.

Beth chose to walk before us, keeping an eye out for anyone who may have been lurking about. Thank goodness no one was roaming about or we would have had a lot of explaining to do, lugging a creature of Hell around the compound. The fiend grew heavy and my arms shook with fatigue by the time we reached the holding chamber. Dr. Wright firmly placed his palm on the hand scanner of the outer door while balancing his end of the fiend in the other. The doors slid open, granting us access to the holding room.

"Will it read my prints as well?"

"You and Evan are the only transporters who have access to the entire building, including all rooms that require print scans."

"Why are we the only two?" I asked as we lugged the monster—who was much heavier than he looked—into the laboratory.

"Several reasons...but mainly because there is no one here to tell you that you can't." His words stung, reminding me I had been abandoned. Dr. Wright didn't mean to hurt me, but what one means to do and actually does are two different things. I surveyed the room, waiting for the tears that brimmed my eyes to dissipate.

"Excuse the appearance of the room," Dr. Wright apologized. "This end of the compound was among the first of the labs to be built and didn't get updated in the expansion," he added, somewhat embarrassed.

He did not mind if his words cut like a whip but cared that we had to enter an out-of-date laboratory. Rolling my eyes, I said nothing.

The room *was* different from the rest of the compound. A putrid green paint coated the walls and a musty odor clung to the air, like a root cellar. To the left was the chamber, an area enclosed by glass on three sides, and to the back, a wall of brick. Inside the chamber a long glass tube extended from the floor to the ceiling. A translucent green substance trapped in between two layers of glass all the way throughout the cylinder—the anti-transporter serum.

My eyes grazed the rest of the room, spotting numerous medical devices, instruments, and computer screens. To the far right, a short wall was adorned with buttons and a speaker box.

"It is so we can communicate," Beth said, pointing to an identical box inside the chamber.

Straight ahead a bed propped up at a ninety-degree angle leered at us. Worn leather straps dangled from its top, middle, and bottom. A shudder rippled through my body at the thought of why those straps were even necessary.

The fiend groaned, and its eyes fluttered. My fear was reflected back at me through Dr. Wright's glasses. With super human speed, Dr. Wright and I wrestled the beast through the chamber and into the glass tube. Not a moment too soon, our fiend regained consciousness. He (I now assumed it was a he) was flaming mad when he became aware he was stuffed into a small glass cylinder.

His red skin glowed vibrantly with rage and the lining around his black lidless eyes lit up with a brilliant shade of yellow. In one smooth motion the tape that bound him was violently ripped apart. His body trembled, and froth flew from his mouth. The fiend banged his head insistently against the glass, calling us every vile name he could think of. Some were—quite creative.

We waited out his fit, which lasted the better part of an hour. Once he was calm, Dr. Wright walked to the speaker, pushed a button, and talked to the fiend. "Hello, my name is Dr. Wright. Can you understand me?"

The fiend's head swiveled, stopping on Dr. Wright. His eyes filled with tears, snot hung in a stringy mess from his nose. He said nothing, instead he stuck out his forked tongue and blew raspberries at Dr. Wright.

Dr. Wright continued, "Listen, we don't want to hurt you. We just need to ask you a few questions."

Again nothing.

I didn't have the patience for this creature. I walked over to the speaker box, pushed Dr. Wright's hand aside, rammed my finger into the talk button, and demanded respect from the vile creature.

"Listen up, you evil spawn of Satan. I'm about three seconds away from cutting your sorry bald head from your scaly shoulders if you don't cooperate. *I am* the transporter you seek. *I am* the one you're trying to keep away from the Cave of Darkness. If you don't answer my questions, I will bring a wrath upon your life that will put your master to shame." My voice trembled, and my nostrils flared. To prevent the fiend from seeing my hands shake I stuffed them into the tiny pockets of my dive suit.

Staring the monster down, I waited for his response. Had I spoken those hate-filled words to a human, they may have had an impact. Of course, his master was the devil himself; I suppose I was nowhere near as frightening as him.

The fiend looked at me, puckered his lips, then burst out laughing hysterically. Maybe I deserved that. He was a blood-thirsty, vile creature and I was a five-foot-two, willowy human with an overabundance of red frizzy hair. There wasn't much about me that was intimidating.

The yellow band around his eyes lit up brighter than before. His laughter set my nerves on edge. I was ready to fly into the holding chamber and give him a beat down. Thank goodness Beth leaned over and whispered in my ear, "He's trying to get a rise out of you. Don't let him distract you from what you need to be doing."

I clenched my jaw, still wanting to knock the monster in his snotty glob but I refrained. "You will do as I say," I commanded smashing my finger onto the talk button again.

"You don't scare me, little girl. Your escape from my master was a fluke; however, if you're stupid enough to go back, you won't be so fortunate, of that I'm sure." The cocky being touched the tips of its index fingers together and pressed them to its lips to unsuccessfully conceal a grin.

My blood boiled. Beth was right, the fiend was trying to bait me, to keep me from my agenda. Grinding my teeth, I spoke calmly. "Okay, have it your way, demon." A dangerous smile climbed up my face. "Tonight, by midnight, your pathetic life will come to a painful end. I have powers you know nothing of. *That* is why I escaped your master, not luck."

I spat the words at the evil thing. "If you don't relent I will make you wish your dear master was the one doling out your punishment." And with those parting words I walked away, the fiend's roaring laughter following me out the door.

Chapter Eight

Report

All the Geeks—including Cassy, Bubba, Evan, and myself—gathered around one of the dining tables for an impromptu meeting to discuss recent events. It had been a horrific twenty-four hours to be sure. Cassy's father being murdered, a fiend being held in a room not far from where we sat, and then of course there was the hectic training schedule I chose to follow leaving me drained.

Dr. Wright cleared his throat loudly, indicating the meeting had come to a start which was unnecessary as none of us had uttered a word since our arrival. "Let's start with Meadow's transport attempt from earlier this morning."

Cassy gave me a cold, hard look. She was furious I would attempt to transport so soon after her father's death. "At 8:15 a.m.," the doctor began, "I was called from the transport room to look at an item of interest which we will discuss momentarily." My ears perked up. In all the excitement, I forgot Dr. Wright had left me alone to go on some secret mission.

"When I returned, apparently Meadow had already transported to Hell and back, returning with a demon. This is huge for several reasons, but we can deduce Meadow is gaining a greater sense of how to manipulate her power. Our next step will be to break down the demon's defenses to gather insight into the Cave of Darkness. If we're successful, Meadow will gain invaluable knowledge for her mission. We just have to be quick as we're now past the timeline we feel is safe for Meadow and her friend, Mark."

Dr. Wright recited his analysis with just as much excitement as one would have going into a twelve-hour session of dental work. It irked my nerves slightly to be spoken of as a science experiment rather than a person but that is all I was to the Geeks.

"Good job, Meadow," Bubba said, his voice emitting a deep understanding, reminding me once again what my friends had endured most of their lives.

"Thanks," I whispered, sending him a reassuring smile. I loved Bubba's heart. He would help hold Cassy and Mrs. Romano together while I worked with the Geeks.

Dr. Wright kept right on talking as if Bubba and I hadn't spoken. "Right now, the fiend is being held in the viewing room. Please don't get too close as he is a foul being. As a matter of fact, we ask that no one access that room unless Dr. Ross or I invite you to do so. We have been interrogating the monster all day, but he hasn't yet broken. However, just as the human soul wanes in the Hell plane, there are changes being made to this creature as well. He's growing weak, and I'm afraid he may not live another twenty-four hours."

Dr. Wright looked over to where the Rosses sat. "Beth, I need you and Will to try your hardest to pinpoint the location of the Cave of Darkness. Contact Ray if you must. The quicker Meadow transports to save Mark, the better."

We all sat quietly, lost in our thoughts, suddenly grasping how very real our situation had become. Lives were at stake—Mark's, mine, and the fiend's.

"Val," Dr. Wright looked at Mrs. Romano. "Cassy," he then turned and looked to my heartbroken friend. The women turned their grief-stricken eyes upon him.

"Hugo was killed in action trying to help the cause. We will never forget the sacrifice he gave for us all. He volunteered to see if he could find what was in Ray Gander's desk because he knew whatever it was would help Meadow in her task. Initially we believed him to be unsuccessful in his mission. However, after talking to our lookouts we found he had in fact made it into the Gander building and back out." Here he paused and pushed his dark-rimmed glasses back up his nose. His gaze shifted to Bubba's mother and father.

"During our examination of his body we found this." Dr. Wright placed a piece of folded parchment on the table directly in front of me.

The frayed scrap of material felt cool in my hands. I unfolded it, aside from the grayish fold marks created by time, the parchment was blank. "What's this?" I asked, puzzled, running my fingers along the four-by-four-inch scrap of material.

"What does it say?" Bubba's mother asked.

"Nothing…nothing at all…it's blank," I said tossing the useless rag back onto the table. Mr. Romano died for a blank piece of trash. *Was this some cruel trick of Ray's, a way to weaken us?* I thought.

"No, something can be uncovered from this parchment. We just have to figure it out. Ray Gander was a highly intelligent man who wouldn't allow easy access to something he believed to be powerful. I'm sure that's part of the reason why this object comes in such a…" Dr. Wright wrinkled his face trying to come up with a fitting word.

"Pitiful scrap of material," I finished.

He nodded in agreement. "Yes, I suppose."

"What do you hope to uncover about this object?" I asked skeptically.

Dr. Wright shrugged his shoulders.

Beth stepped up and looked closely at the object and echoed Dr. Wright's sentiments. "Ray Gander—although an evil man—was brilliant. Whatever this is, he wouldn't ask you to get it unless it was useful or powerful. I know he's evil, Meadow, but he cares for his family even if he shows it in odd ways. Satan could have destroyed his soul for helping you or given him a punishment worse than what he already endures."

I nodded my head—not so much because I agreed with what Beth said but because I didn't want to have this conversation. I also didn't care how Ray was punished. All I knew was Ray Gander was the man who put me in this situation and ruined my life. Now I was left to navigate the caves of Hell to save the boy I cared for or die by the hands of Satan and his cronies. To say the least, I wasn't a big fan of Ray Gander at the moment.

"Meadow, do you mind if we study the parchment and see what we can unearth?" Dr. Ross asked, already reaching for the scrap of material.

"Sure," I answered, shaking my head.

Dr. Ross studied me for a moment. "In the meantime, you can try and contact Ray as well, see if he will tell you anything important." I puckered my lips and nodded. Ray was the last person I wanted to speak to, but it had to be done.

"Okay, now that we have that cleared up, we have something else to discuss and it won't be welcoming news at all." Dr. Wright looked down at me, a great pain and sadness radiating from his gaze. He cut his eyes away, avoiding the questioning look I was shooting his way and pretending the paperwork before him suddenly became interesting. Whatever news he was about to deliver was going to shake us all.

"Last night the Parkers went with Hugo Romano as his backup." Dr. Wright paused to look over at Richard and Mallory Parker, once again weighing each word he spoke with precision.

The Parkers wrapped their arms around each other. I loved the Parkers; they were incredibly kind and loyal people. Although very fit and athletic, they were also very tiny people, unlike their gentle giant son. It made sense they were the lookouts for Mr. Romano.

"Richard monitored the north side of the Gander building and Mallory the southwest. Being strategically located as they were, Hugo could be seen from all angles."

"Wait, this was a planned trip? I'm confused," I blurted out. I needed to make whatever news was about to unfold stop. I didn't want to hear the details of how Mr. Romano had been killed.

Dr. Wright shifted uncomfortably, pulling his glasses from his face to clean them on his lab coat and then replacing them. "It wasn't a planned trip at all. However, the Parkers were on lookout duty for the compound. They figured out what Hugo was doing and confronted him as he climbed into his Jeep. They formulated a plan to meet him at the Gander building as backup just in case..."

A low sniffling came from Mrs. Parker, but I didn't tear my eyes away from Dr. Wright. "Hugo made it to the Gander building before the Parkers and went inside, knowing his comrades would soon arrive. By the time Richard and Mallory secured their hiding spots, they saw who they believed to be Hugo Romano run into the Gander building. Unfortunately, minutes later two figures emerged from the building. The Parkers realized, too late, they had been terribly mistaken."

Dr. Wright's voice broke and tiny droplets of tears peeked out from under his glasses but still he read from his papers and didn't look up.

"Richard used his two-way radio instructing Mallory to stand down. She obeyed his orders and looked on as Richard ran to help Hugo in what appeared to be a deadly struggle."

Gruff sobbing broke from Mr. Parker's chest, and my heart pounded more quickly with each word that was spoken. "Richard made it to the two men just as the blade wielded by the attacker sunk into Hugo's chest, the man then fled. Hugo fell to the ground, and Richard pursued the attacker. Richard tackled the perpetrator from behind. He then grabbed the ski mask on the attacker's face and yanked it off the man's head to reveal none other than…"

Collectively the room held its breath in anticipation of who could have committed such a horrible crime. Whoever it was would pay for what they had taken from us. They would regret the day they ever heard the name—

"…Mike Fields." Dr. Wright's words cut through my heart. I wasn't ready. *My dad—Mike Fields—a murderer? Mike Fields…did he say…Mike…* The name lost its meaning. My body went numb, yet my heart raged inside of my chest. The air in the room grew stagnant.

All eyes turned to me, looks of shock and pity weighed me down. Stop looking, please stop looking. Didn't they know their stares killed a piece of my heart? My eyes sought the only person in this room that mattered to me—Cassy. Her beautiful dark red-rimmed eyes filled with shock. My cheeks burned with regret for who I was, who my parents were. I stood, the room spun.

My legs shook and wobbled as I ran. The thumping of my black commando boots echoed through the halls. My first thought was to leave for good but if spotted, I could get everyone killed. Instead, I went to my living quarters and lay on my bed and cried. I cried until my throat was raw, until there were no more tears, only the bitter, dry hacking of my sobs filling the room.

What happened to my perfect little life? My mother was a psychopath, my grandfather a demon from Hell, and my father a murderer. I wondered if it would ever end. Or, a better question, how it would end? *Lord God, where are You? Certainly not among this mess or I would see some sliver of You here. Yet, I'm alone.*

Chapter Nine

Unwanted Truth

Exhaustion settled in. I prayed my eyes would never open in this world again. Just as I dozed off, the sound of my entry door sliding open woke me from the threshold of sleep. The fact that anyone could casually drop into my living space was maddening. Stomping into my bathroom, I slammed the door behind me. Taking my time, I splashed warm water on my face and neck. Scrubbing my face softly at first, then forcefully attempting to wash away the pain that clung to every inch of me.

Maybe whoever walked in would take a hint and leave. But they didn't, and what made it worse was the person who came to visit was the last person on Earth I wanted to see. Well, he was in the top five.

"Oh no, I'm not in the mood for you. You need to leave! I really can't do this with you right now." I pointed at the front door. Frantically, I looked around the room for something hard to throw at his head.

"Okay, okay." He held his hands in front of himself. "I will, as soon as I say what I should have said a long time ago," Evan said hotly. His temper was an even match for my own.

"Now? After everything that has taken place in the last twenty-four hours, you choose now? There is nothing you can say to change how I feel about you." I crossed my arms over my chest and gave him the death stare.

"Listen, I know the timing is terrible, but in light of what happened I have to tell you now. We're living in dangerous times, and I may never get the chance to speak to you again."

"You mean in case I die?"

He nodded. "We're all in danger, Meadow. You're not in this alone. All of us here have given up our lives for you. Some of us may still lose our lives; some already have." His voice held no contempt. The honesty I once loved about him irked me now.

I was tired, hurt, and somewhat curious about what he wanted to share with me. "Fine, say what you need to, then leave." He had given up his life for me after all.

"What if I told you, you broke my heart well before I broke yours?" he asked.

My jaw dropped, and I curled my tiny hands into fists ready to punch his lights out. "Are you kidding me?" I snarled, slapping my hand down on the table, causing him to wince. "I was good to you, no I was amazing... I gave you my heart. I loved you and you...you..." In my rage the words would no longer come from my mouth. I wondered if my words even mattered. They were nothing more than the ramblings of a broken-hearted school girl.

My shoulders shook and all I could do was cry. Earlier I believed I had cried myself out but apparently, I was wrong. What Evan was doing—trying to turn the table on me—it was unfair. *After all that I have been through, he comes here to blame me for the demise of our relationship?*

Evan cautiously walked over to me and wrapped me in his arms. Going against my true feelings, I melted into his embrace. It felt good to be in his arms again, to have someone hold me, to reassure me that I was okay.

I allowed myself to indulge in those feelings for a few moments before I broke away. It was time to be strong. The material of my suit scraped my face as I raked away the infernal tears that insisted on fleeing from my eyes. I wondered if there would ever be an end to these tears for me and my friends.

Evan's brown eyes filled with remorse as he spoke. "It was my senior year, and I had been training with the Geeks for years. At that point we weren't sure if we would ever have to use our training, but the Geeks made sure we understood one day our lives may depend on having the skills they taught us—*your life* would depend on it. Bubba, Cassy, and I had to be ready to defend you even if it meant our death."

To the death? A surreal feeling washed over me. *How much of their lives had they given up for me?* As I lived this normal, carefree life, my best friends lived a lie. *How could I repay them for their sacrifice? Do I even have to?* I had never asked for any of this. And given the option, I would have gladly learned to defend myself. A small voice in my head reminded me that they didn't ask for this either.

"You have no idea how it felt knowing your girlfriend was being hunted by crazy scientists ready to do anything to catch her. It's crazy you know, and so...hard." Evan looked at me, his dark eyes melting my hardened heart. "There were days I didn't want to let you out of my sight because the thought of something happening to you tore me up inside." I scoffed. He didn't seem too concerned when he was in his dorm with Long-Legs McGee.

"Seriously listen," Evan pleaded. "Before graduation the Geeks decided Cassy and Bubba were ready to watch over you when I left for college. They were fully trained, and Dr. Wright said I was off the hook, if I wanted. Cass and Bubba were more than enough manpower to protect you, they're a lethal duo. Especially Cassy..."

Cassy? Bubba? Lethal...

"I told Dr. Wright I would just wait and see what happened. I had fallen for you, Meadow, and no matter how many times I thought about leaving, I couldn't imagine my life without you."

He brushed his fingers along the side of my face. I closed my eyes trying to pretend he hadn't deceived me with the beautiful leggy blonde beauty almost a year ago. But he had, and the image of the two of them together haunted me. His deception was too much to bear, even now.

"I had been at State University for about six weeks, my last visit home before we split up... I overheard my parents talking. Mom always liked you, Meadow, but there was always something...she didn't approve of our relationship."

My mouth dropped open. I cared about Evan's entire family a great deal. To think his mother didn't want me with her son drove the knife of betrayal straight through my chest.

"They were on the back porch—Mom and Dad—in a heated discussion. You know they never fight so I was intrigued and eavesdropped. I heard Mom say to Dad, 'You know if Meadow ever successfully transports, it will be to save her soulmate, her true love. That means one of two things has to happen. Either Evan has to be in Hell for Meadow to save him or Evan isn't her soulmate at all.' She said she couldn't stand to see the heartbreak I would endure because those idiots felt the need to see this horrific experiment through."

"But...I..." Evan's mother had always been so kind and loving to me. I couldn't believe what I was hearing. And I had no idea what to think about this true love, soulmate business.

"So, when I say you broke my heart before I broke yours, that is true. Only you didn't know it. The first day you told me you were having dreams I was afraid you were already thinking of him, that maybe he was calling to you. The boy in the cave...maybe I should have talked to you about being a transporter, or maybe I should have told the Geeks, but jealousy took the driver's seat to any good sense I may have had. Eventually, I shared with Cassy and she promised to keep an eye out for signs that may have indicated you had transported."

"Why wouldn't you say—" I started.

"I hated him," Evan shouted into the room scaring me, "whoever he was. I hoped you would never transport to him and maybe one day...one day you would be free to love me."

"So, you knew someone from Hell may be calling to me, yet you did nothing? In what world does that make sense?"

"Look, we know Satan's crafty. He tempted me with that other girl knowing I was in a bad place. He made me feel alone and that no one cared. That's when Sara...I mean she...came into the picture."

Sara. She had a name, and hearing it fall from his lips so familiarly, as if he'd said it many times, tore at my soul.

"One of the worst things you could have done to me..." I needed to shift gears, and I wanted to know why he thought I deserved to be punished.

"I tried to make myself see you weren't so important; that I could replace you and be fine. But I wasn't. There's no one like you, Meadow. I will spend the rest of my life trying to earn your forgiveness."

"You really loved me?" I asked, searching his face for any sign that he was lying.

"I still do." He reached over and grabbed my wrist. The feel of his thumb running over the top of my hand caused a shiver to run through my body. "But, we believe this Mark guy," he added then paused and clenched his jaw for a moment, "could be your soulmate."

"It doesn't make sense. Dr. Wright told me you and I transported together when we were mere infants. Who's to say we aren't soulmates? Or that this whole soulmate thing isn't hogwash?"

"Because you never transported again until Mark was in distress. And you're *my* true love, Meadow, so I was able to tolerate the transport when we were babies because you were by my side."

There seemed to be some holes in his logic, but he still had my hand and thoughts of our past swirled through my mind.

"Why would no one share this information with me?" I would have a talk with the Geeks once I made it back from Hell with Mark. There could be no more secret keeping. *Did this mean Cassy and Bubba weren't soulmates and that is why they couldn't transport?*

"The Geeks think you should go into this with facts and figures. They don't believe what my parents say about you transporting to save your true love. Mom swears that's what Ray told her, but of course I've heard he isn't always truthful."

His cheeks turned red and he looked slightly embarrassed. "I'm telling you this because I know you're a spiritual and emotional being. I also know you do your best work when you're passionate about something. The only way you will save Mark is to wear your heart on your sleeve. I know you'll fight harder for him if you know there may be a deeper connection between the two of you."

Evan dropped my hand and turned to leave but I grabbed his arm, stopping him. "Thank you for sharing that with me. You're right. I will fight harder."

His head drooped as he walked away, his apology freeing me from the bondage of his betrayal. Now I had to formulate a plan to save Mark, bring him back, and keep him on Earth with me.

Chapter Ten

A Fiend's Tale

Evan left, and I finished getting ready. It was almost time for dinner so there was no time for that nap after all. I had just changed into fresh training gear when Beth entered my room.

No privacy.

"The fiend wants to talk but he'll only speak to you," Beth said breathing hard. She gripped her injured shoulder, her face scrunched in a tight grimace.

"Let's see what he has to say." I smiled grimly at Beth and followed her into the corridor.

"You doing okay?" She asked, glancing at me from the corner of her eye.

"As well as can be expected." I shrugged not wanting to share with her how *not okay* I truly was. At some point, my moment would come and I would have a total freak-out. I was way too calm for a girl who just hours before had been informed her dad had killed her best friend's father.

"Here you are," Beth said, stopping at the door of the viewing room. "I have to check on Val and Cassy. Dr. Wright and the Parkers are inside waiting for you."

"Thanks." I gently placed my hand to the print scanner and the doors slid open.

My eyes shifted to the fiend. Immediately I could see he was dying. His skin had turned a muddy shade of brown and his eyes had lost their luster.

The creature's elf-shaped ears drooped like a scalded dog, his mouth sagged to one side. My heart skipped a beat before it dropped to my stomach. Even if this creature was evil, seeing him suffer was difficult.

Pulling in a deep breath, I walked to the intercom. "Are you ready to talk?" I asked with as much bravery as I could.

His dry, cracked lips parted and he croaked, "Yes, but only because I will be doing the Dark One a favor. Once you enter the Cave of Darkness you will never come out." The fiend's attempt at laughter turned into a hacking coughing fit, leaving him breathless.

"Okay, where's the cave?" I asked once the creature was able to breathe.

"The stairs…the rock stairs leading straight down the ravine…to the entrance…" an audible wheezing followed each word the monster spoke. "…to the Cave of Darkness... You will be submerged into a complete and total cursed blackness. If you're lucky enough to find your friend, you won't be so fortunate finding your way out." The fiend's dead eyes found joy in my discomfort.

"What dangers are in the cave?" I asked.

"Your own madness is enough but there are creatures of the darkness even I wouldn't go near." The fiend shivered at his own words. His fear compelled me to believe I may not make it out of the cave at all.

"What do you mean, my own madness?"

"The darkness will drive you mad, even if you're a strong-minded redheaded brat. The darkness is alive and will pry into your mind forcing you to face your own personal hell." The fiend shook violently, his body slumped inside the cylinder that held him prisoner.

"Wait," I pressed the button, hoping the being was still alive. "How do I find Mark?" I cried. The creature's face pressed against the glass. He didn't stir, nor did he hear me. He was dead.

My heart thumped in my chest, another death added to my conscience. The only way to stop the death and destruction that plagued those around me was to save Mark and show the Devil I wouldn't back down until I fulfilled what God had in store for me—whatever that may be.

"We need to dispose of the body," I said hardening my heart to make it through what needed to be done.

"We'll take care of him, but we need to examine him first." Dr. Wright said. "Dr. Ross wants to see you as soon as you're free. I believe he has some information on the parchment found in Ray's desk."

"If you have this under control, I will head over there now. I plan on transporting in the morning and I need any help I can get."

"Go, we're good here," Dr. Wright responded, a look of disgust covering his face as he looked at the dead fiend's paling figure. He turned to the Parkers and described how they were to "take care" of the fiend's body.

I left before hearing the disturbing details. It took a few minutes to find Dr. Ross because he was in the micro lab on the other side of the compound. The lab held several microscopes on a long counter the length of the narrow room. I found him closely examining the piece of parchment under a microscope that Mr. Romano had unearthed from Gander's.

"Dr. Ross," I said, approaching his stooped figure.

"Oh, Meadow, good you're here." He pulled away from the microscope and straightened up to greet me.

"Dr. Wright said you had some information about the parchment for me," I said, eyeing the object warily.

"Yes and no." Dr. Ross's eyes lit up. "You see I know what it is, but I don't know what it does or even how it works."

"Oh," I said dully, wondering how he could muster up so much excitement about a scrap of fabric. "What is it?"

"If I'm correct, this is the Mezirot you heard the fiends speak of. Beth found an old journal of Ray's and he describes the Mezirot as a remnant of an ancient artifact to which he added some sort of biological agent that reacts with the transporter serum. He doesn't explain what that reaction may be or how it works; however, that could be because he created the Mezirot many years after the transporters went into hiding."

My voice squeaked, "The Mezirot…" I licked my lips, cleared my throat, and tried again.

"The Mezirot…what did I hear the fiends say…" *It was powerful…why can't I think? I need to talk to Ray.*

"Do the Geeks have any information?"

"I'm afraid not. I have asked everyone. At this point the only person who could give you the answers you seek is Ray."

"Ray," I whispered his name. I wondered if he would even help me. In the best of times he was fickle and quite impossible to deal with.

Contemplating how to handle Ray, I chewed on the inside of my cheek, an old nervous trait that had re-manifested itself since living underground. "I will try tonight. It's easier to connect when there are no distractions."

"Meadow, how are you? Are you okay?" Dr. Ross asked me, his kind face furrowed in concern.

I opened my mouth to assure him I was okay, but instead the moment had come for me to have my breakdown. "No, Dr. Ross, I'm far from okay."

And for the next hour, I rattled off every fear and frustration that had been bubbling within me. Through tears and bursts of anger, I shared my fears on how my heart had changed and that I was deathly afraid of being stuck in the Cave of Darkness forever.

Then there was how alienated I felt from everyone else. In my heart I felt personally responsible for the death of Mr. Romano and the demon. Cassy would come to hate me, maybe Bubba as well. My parents were traitors, and Evan was heavier baggage than I was ready to contend with.

To his credit Dr. Ross listened intently until I was talked out. "You know, Meadow, tonight before you go to sleep, I think you should spend some time with God. We, the Geeks..." he smiled at the nickname Cassy had donned them with. "...we have pushed you and filled your head with talk of fighting, Hell, and science mumbo jumbo. We have trained you to be a demon-killing machine."

I snickered knowing I was far from a killing machine. "We have done nothing but shove pretty harsh stuff into your mind, but we have forgotten your strongest power is the relationship you have with God. If you lose your relationship with Him, you won't succeed in your mission."

"It's hard to talk with Him when I don't understand how He could let this happen to me."

"We may never know what God had planned for you before evil wormed its way into all of our lives, but I do know He instilled within you gifts that can overcome the pits of Hell. Don't forget, there is no part of evil that ever truly wins when we allow God in. He has already won."

"Yeah," I replied miserably.

Dr. Ross placed his hands on my shoulders. "Please don't forget that this world isn't the good stuff. There is something much more amazing waiting for us. This stuff here," he waved his hand around indicating the compound, "it's all temporary."

The memory of my brief visit to heaven came to mind. Dr. Ross's words echoed what the sweet angel revealed when I was there. And there was something sweeter still—home.

My heavenly home was waiting for me when it was time. I thought about how beautiful my tiny glimpse of heaven was and how badly I didn't want to leave. Even if I were killed in Hell, I still won. Failure wasn't on the table. To live is gain, to die is gain—what an awesome thought.

Dr. Ross was right. I hadn't been spending as much time with God as I should have. To be honest I was spending *no* time with Him. It hurt knowing that the girl I had been several months ago, who had been so strong in Christ, had slipped away.

Dr. Ross wrapped his arm around my shoulders. Hanging my head, I cried as he consoled me. I was so consumed in my grief, I didn't notice Cassy's presence in the room until she wedged herself between us.

"It's okay, doll. Everything is going to be okay," Cassy whispered words of encouragement. Guilt grew inside me as my friend held me close. I should have been consoling her, not the other way around.

At some point Dr. Ross disappeared, leaving the two of us alone. When we broke apart, I tried to apologize for my behavior and for what my father had done.

"Cassy, I'm so sorry...so sorry. How can you ever forgive me?"

But Cassy wouldn't hear of it. Her voice wavered as she spoke. "We're confused, scared, and hurt, but none of this is your fault. You have nothing to be sorry about. This life..." she choked on her words and looked away. "...this life was thrust upon us all. We never had a choice. Since the beginning we have been family. I love you and I'm so...so proud of what you're doing. I only wish I could be there to help you kick some demon butt."

The look in Cassy's eyes made me laugh. I believed she would love nothing more than to ninja-kick a fiend right in the kisser. This side of my friend was new to me, but I was glad she was now able to share more of who she really was.

"Thank you." I leaned the side of my head against hers.

Her stomach growled astronomically loud. We both giggled and for a split second it was like it was before—me and my best friend together sharing a laugh, ready for a new adventure. Except this adventure was deadly, and we may not make it out alive. The thought sobered me quickly.

"Come on. We need to grab dinner. The Geeks have likely snagged the good stuff by now." Cassy grabbed my hand and pulled me along, she too, realizing the darkness that surrounded us but not yet ready to give up hope.

Smiling at my friend, I squeezed her hand as we walked to the dining hall together. My heart was much lighter knowing Cassy didn't blame me for what my father had done.

Chapter Eleven

The Mezirot

Lying on my bed I closed my eyes in an attempt to speak to God. "God...um I know I have uh...been absent lately and I'm sorry...it's just I haven't felt Your presence." *Should I really be turning this around on God?* "I mean not that it's Your fault; I'm sure it's mine somehow..." *Or is it because I was given a super crappy life that is beyond my control?*

No matter how I started, the bitterness of abandonment would creep into my words, driving that wedge between myself and God even further. When I was growing up, my pastor once said that we as humans sometimes do too much talking; when we would fare better by being silent and meditating on the Word that God gave us.

I found myself reaching for the little Bible someone had the foresight to place on my bedside table. Opening its delicately thin pages, I allowed God to speak. And speak to me He did in the words of Ephesians 6:12-13:

> *For our struggle is not against flesh and blood, but against the rulers, against the authorities, against the powers of this dark world, and against the spiritual forces of evil in heavenly realms. Therefore, put on the full armor of God, so that when the day of evil comes, you may be able to stand your ground, and after you have done everything, to stand.*

This passage reminded me I needed to be equipped with the armor of God because there is strength in His truth. My heart would be protected with the breastplate of righteousness. I could fit my feet with readiness from the gospel of peace. The shield of faith, the helmet of salvation, and the sword of the Spirit would guard me from the enemy's attack and defeat the evil in my path.

God knew my soul needed those words and they gave me a renewed sense of strength. Now I felt strong enough to move on to my next task, which would be to sweet-talk information out of Ray.

"Ray…" I concentrated as hard as I could to reach him. "Ray." I had been calling his name in my mind for around thirty minutes, but he wasn't answering. Either he couldn't hear me, or he didn't care to respond. Either way I had to sleep as the next day was going to be the biggest challenge I would have to face.

*   *   *

Dr. Ross brought the Mezirot to me early the next morning. It sat on my bedside table where I stared at it, fearful of what powers it held. Cautiously, I picked it up, allowing my fingers to explore the rough fabric. One last time I called out to Ray.

"What do you want, child?" He finally asked gruffly.

"Sorry…did I disturb you from torturing the souls of the innocent?" I asked sarcastically.

"Funny, no I don't have that pleasure, but if I did, I know who would be first on my list," he grumbled.

"I have the…the Mezirot. Could this ratty rag be what you wanted me to get out of your desk?"

Ray cackled in delight. "Ah, you're braver than I thought."

"No, not—it wasn't me. Hugo Romano lost his life for this piece of trash. My father killed him."

"Quite unfortunate. Hugo was one of the good ones." Ray muttered.

"How did my father know where to look?" I asked.

"Your mother, undoubtedly. I'm sure she informed your father to keep an eye out for the old Gander crew, especially in times such as these."

"Who knew of its location?"

"I alone knew the location of the Mezirot until I divulged it to you and, of course, I didn't reveal to you what it was in case there was a rogue scientist amongst you."

"What does the Mezirot do?"

"Ah," Ray cackled. "My favorite experiment outside of the transporter…then again the Mezirot and the transporter go hand-in-hand."

59

Ray's voice rang with pride.

"What do you mean? Ray, be straight with me. I have little time here." I checked the time on my alarm clock.

"Well, if you're in such a hurry, maybe I should leave you alone," Ray huffed. My elderly demon grandfather behaved like a toddler when he didn't get his way.

"No, no, no don't. I'm sorry. I'm just tired and a little grumpy...please, I need your help."

"Hmm, ungrateful kids nowadays," Ray grumbled. "Anyway, the Mezirot will be of great use to you in the Cave of Darkness. It's one of very few objects that will cut through the wretched darkness in that cave..." Ray sounded hesitant.

"What? What are you not telling me?" I asked.

"The Mezirot doesn't work for long in that environment and your ability to see isn't great. It's kind of like the moment you walk into a dark room after spending time outside on an extremely sunny day. Don't get me wrong. It's better than nothing, but I was never able to perfect its function in that regard."

"How do I get it to work? So far it's been pretty useless."

"To get the Mezirot to work, wrap your hand around it and channel your strength into it as you do when you speak to me. The serum in your blood will create a reaction, lighting it up temporarily. Keep in mind, the Mezirot will lose its power if used for a prolonged amount of time."

"I will take any help I can get," I thought to Ray.

"You still plan on coming back for the boy, huh?" He asked.

"I do," I answered.

Ray tsked loudly in my mind. "Then there is something you should know. I'm sure you haven't yet heard. It seems your mother has found her way down here—for good." For once Ray's voice wasn't filled with joy at someone else's expense. He sounded almost—sad.

"She is...is she dead?" I asked.

"I'm sorry, kid," he answered.

My mother was dead, another casualty of this sick and twisted war. My heart sank. Secretly I had hoped my story would have a happy ending. Mom and Dad would change their ways, the Geeks would forgive them, and we would all live happily ever after. But that was just a sad delusion. Those thoughts were nothing more than my inner naive self, wishing for the impossible.

"You still there, kid?" Ray asked.

"Yeah, I'm here," I answered, shaking the thoughts from my head. *Strange,* I thought, *that Mr. Romano's death stung more than my own mother's.* Surely that would be another issue to work through with my psychiatrist Dr. Barnes after this mess was over. Maybe I would make an appointment, but I knew he would have me committed for sure if I shared with him the events of the last few weeks.

"You must be careful. Nancy is being shunned because she failed to keep you in Hell. However, if she can get her hands on you, she won't hesitate to turn you over to the Dark One. Also, if you get stuck in the Cave of Darkness, you can go—"

"Insane, yeah I know." I sighed, defeated. No matter how ready I was to battle the demons of Hell, I wasn't ready to have a meeting with my mother. *How could I defend myself against her?*

"One more question," I said.

"Just one?" Ray asked rudely.

Ignoring his surliness, I asked something that had bothered me since Evan and I last spoke. "Evan told me the only way to successfully transport was to find your soulmate. Is that true?"

"He must be referring to the conversation I had with his mother many years ago, she was always a dense one. True love, yes. Soulmate not so much…but…it's complicated. I can't go over that with you now as it would take more time than we have." He was right. Eventually, I would get the answers I needed, but now I needed to worry about Mark.

"Thank you for helping me."

There was a slight pause. "Don't lose the Mezirot. It has more powers than I can reveal right now but always, always keep it close. You would be wise to not let such a powerful object fall into the hands of Satan or his fiends."

"I won't. Thanks again." I pulled my thoughts back to myself and felt Ray's presence leave me.

With thoughts of my mother, father, Mark, and Ray swirling through my mind I decided it was time to get moving. Mark needed me now and there was nothing I could do about the losses that continued to happen except for pray we would find a way to end this madness before we lost any more.

Chapter Twelve

Mixed Feelings

Despair hung in the air and my chest grew heavy with each passing moment. Cassy, Bubba, Evan, and the Geeks surrounded my cot. Anxiety gripped me in a way it hadn't in years. I was unsure if I could do this at all but then I thought of Mark. Mark and his sweet innocent smile, his piercing blue eyes, and his gentle way that kept me grounded.

"You ready, Meadow?" Dr. Wright asked. I gave just the slightest of nods, yes.

The Geeks and I had trained hard for the last week, but I was far from ready. It would be a miracle if I found Mark and brought him back unscathed.

Clenching my jaw, I nodded my head with more conviction. "Ready."

"You have less than twelve hours to find Mark and make it back to us. Anything over that and we don't know what will happen."

"Okay…well um…guys it's hard to…transport with all of you watching me. So…can you take a hike?" I asked.

Nervous laughter filled my ears as everyone except for Evan, Cassy, Dr. Wright, and Beth exited the room. Dr. Wright and Beth would stay with my body while I was gone. Cassy and Evan hovered over me, neither moving. Sighing, I swung my legs over the edge of the cot and looked up at the pair.

"Be careful. I would go in your place if I could." Cassy hugged me tight. I wrapped my arms around her a little tighter and hung on.

Desperately, I wanted to tell her about my mother, but I was afraid of her reaction. Mostly I didn't want anyone to feel sorry for me, to show me pity. Not for the loss of a woman who wanted me dead. When this mess was over, I would tell them.

"I'm sorry, Cass," I whispered to her. She shook her head and pulled back to look me straight in the eye.

"Don't be sorry, be safe." Cassy put on her brave face.

"I love you." I squeezed her hands in mine.

"I love you too, my sister." She hugged me one last time then made a quick exit.

Through the door's window I watched Cassy run to Bubba and fling herself into his arms. My eyes glazed over as I watched Bubba wrap Cassy in his massive biceps, wishing I had that with someone. I had been too cautious with Mark, too scared of my own heart.

"I know what you're thinking." Evan's voice broke through my thoughts. He lightly placed his hand on my shoulder.

"Not so long ago I wished that were you and me." I turned to face him. Evan was the image of most girls' dreams. He was built, tall, had perfect teeth, and big brown puppy dog eyes that gave him a boyish appearance.

"Me too," Evan said softly.

"I'm sorry, Evan…everything is messed up and there are so many uncertainties…half-truths…lies…uncharted territory. I don't know what or how I feel."

Evan took a step closer to me, forcing me to look either at his face or his broad muscular chest. Just the thought made my skin grow hot, and I knew my face was lit up like a Christmas tree, ornate with a generous dusting of freckles.

"There's only one way to find out," he whispered, lowering his head to mine.

Is he going to kiss me? Should I let him?

"How?" I was certain the thud of my heart concealed the audible gulp that traveled down my esophagus.

Evan hesitated, then pulled back and shook his head. "You have to save him. If there's truly nothing between you two, I'll be here." He leaned back into me. I closed my eyes and treasured the feel of his lips against my forehead. "Be careful," he whispered in my ear. A shiver ran down my back as I closed my eyes and nodded. My eyes didn't open until I heard the door shut behind him, leaving me alone with Dr. Wright and Beth.

My cheeks instantly flushed with embarrassment; I had completely forgotten their presence in the room. "I'm ready for real this time." *Ready to melt through the floor.* I laid back down on my cot and stared straight ahead, not willing to look at either of them.

"Are you sure you want to go through with this?" Beth asked.

"She has to and you know it," Dr. Wright said impatiently, almost angry.

Sometimes Dr. Wright could be insensitive, but he was right. I had no choice in the matter. Mark had to be saved. So much time had gone by I was certain he had suffered tremendously, more than I could imagine.

Beth opened her mouth to argue but I cut in, "I'm sure."

Pushing Evan from my mind I focused on Mark. This time I transported within a matter of seconds. Strange how the thought of Mark could send me back so quickly. Without a doubt there was a special bond between us. I wondered if he really was my soulmate—if true love really worked this way, like some fairytale.

Shaking the thought from my mind I studied the area. Conveniently I had transported to the landing between the Water Cave and the Fire Cave, my go-to spot. There was a narrow rocky ledge on each side of the gorge. The only way to either side was to cross a heavy flat rock which lay over the top of the canyon that divided the Water Cave and the Fire Cave.

Spinning deliberately on my heels, I searched for who might be on guard waiting for me. My stomach drew into a tight ball as I saw that not only was there one fiend guarding the stairwell to the Cave of Darkness, there were four. Satan was prepared for my return. Oddly enough, the idiots were fighting over who was going to kill me and how they were going to do it.

"I'm gonna dip her into the river of fire and listen to her scream." One of the fiends giggled evilly.

"Oh yeah, I'm going to eat her alive and pick my teeth with her bones." The next one cackled, sending the group into uncontrollable laughter.

"You're all stupid," the largest fiend said dumbly. "I will give her to master and be rewarded beyond anyone else in this wretched place." The other fiends stopped cackling and listened to their ringleader.

Nimbly, I skulked behind them, but their laughter stopped, no longer concealing my footsteps.

"Hey," the large one said, sniffing the air.

Can it smell me?

"Do you sme—"

Yup, he can.

Not one to wait, I sprung on the bulky fiend's back. The spunky thing bucked and ran around like a wild turkey. I hung on for dear life but my body began to slide off the monster's back.

Missing no opportunities, I kicked one of the smaller fiends in the back of the head, knocking him to the ground. The fiend I was attached to flipped me over his shoulders, landing me hard on my back. A sharp rock pierced my skin next to my spine. Greedily I gulped air into my lungs, failing to divert my mind from the pain as my spine burned with fire.

The fiend flung his tall reptilian body over top of me. I kicked him in the chest with both feet just in time. He sprawled backwards, tripping two of his buddies who had pounced in our direction. Ray told me these guys were dim, and he was right; however, they were strong and dumb which made them a dangerous combo.

Out of the corner of my eye, I caught the flash of the fourth fiend running towards the rock bridge leading to the Fire Cave. If he alerted Satan of my presence, I would never make it to Mark.

Ignoring the empty space under the rocky bridge which typically paralyzed me with fear, I sprinted across. Just as the beast was about to enter the tunnel to the Fire Cave, I dove at his feet and encircled his legs with my arms.

The fiend went down; kicking, screaming, and clawing. "Ahhhhh, get off me you wretched girl!" The little devil landed a kick to my face with the heel of its foot, I heard a crack. Instantly, my mouth tasted of copper, and I spit out a stream of blood. The fiend and I both scrambled to our feet.

"You... won't... win," I struggled to pull in a breath.

"I don't have to," the monster shot back nastily.

What does that mean? To cover my confusion, I laughed in the fiend's face and spit another mouthful of blood at its feet.

The fiend's nose wrinkled in disgust. "You will fit in well down here," he croaked.

"I don't plan on staying," I shot back.

"We'll see," the fiend threatened, crouching in attack stance. Circling each other slowly we anticipated one another's move. He studied my stance and the way I held myself. I would have to strike first, but I needed to do something he wouldn't expect, and I needed to do it quickly.

The fiend's eyes shifted just past me and it smiled. The sound of bare feet scraping across the gritty stone prickled my senses. Once again, I found myself at an unfair disadvantage. Pretending not to notice the approaching predator, I moved closer to my adversary.

Looking deeply into its shiny bulbous eyes, I made out the reflection of the second sneaky monster creeping up behind me. The tiniest shift of energy in the air pulled at my strength. Closing my eyes, I fought the wave of energy-sapping nausea that accompanied the presence of fiends. Heat radiated from the fiend behind me.

Without warning I jumped straight in the air, pouncing on the fiend's stomach. The force of the impact projected me into the air, allowing me to plant a roundhouse kick to the second fiend straight in its temple. It never saw it coming. The brute's eyes rolled back in its head as it soared over the rocky ledge down into the gorge below. Mouth wide open, I watched as the fiend flailed in the air, its blood curling scream ricocheting off my eardrums.

The remaining fiends took advantage of the moment, grabbing my arms on either side and hoisting me to my feet. The third fiend walked towards me menacingly, a sneer crossing its reptilian face. The skin on its hand made a crackling sound as it tightened its fist.

The fiend was merciless, the evil glint in his eyes radiating a sick twisted joy at my pain. The speed in which the blows were delivered was unlike anything I could have imagined. Left, right, left, right, the fiend drew back again and again. My eyes rolled back in their sockets, my soul would only take so much more before I was knocked unconscious or killed.

An image of Beth and Dr. Wright performing life-saving support on my dying body popped into my mind. *How would they feel if I died within minutes of my transport? What would happen to Mark if I died now? It isn't going to happen—not yet and most certainly not by these creeps.*

As the fiend tightened its spindly fingers into a tight fist preparing to land what I knew would be a devastating blow, I used my remaining strength to swing the two fiends attached to my arms straight forward. The energy behind that motion smashed the unsuspecting fiend in front of me on either side. All three of the creatures fell to the ground in one unconscious clump of red-skinned evil.

"Well…that was unexpected." My voice broke through the deathly quiet room. A crazed giggle burst from my mouth. "Ugh, why am I so crazy? I need to stop being stupid and think. What do I do here?"

Their bodies needed to be hidden. If another fiend walked by, I would be found out. There was nothing for me to do but dump them over the cliff like their buddy. I made quick work of rolling each fiend over the edge, grateful I couldn't hear the thump of their bodies hitting the bottom. Once the last fiend was gone, I scrambled to the stairwell descending to the Cave of Darkness.

Chapter Thirteen

Descent into the Dark

The jagged stairway was incredibly steep and more dangerous than I originally suspected. Awkwardly I clambered down the dilapidated steps, carefully avoiding loose rocks. Fighting the fiends had zapped my strength, making the treacherous journey insufferable.

After I had traveled halfway down the chasm, I looked up. Standing that far below the surface put into perspective how massive the cave system really was. A faint line of light from above illuminated the way but with each step I took, the light dwindled.

Around and around the corkscrew staircase circled in upon itself until my head grew dizzy. Each step more crooked, uneven, and crumbly than the one before it. The trip took so much longer than I believed possible. Fear of how little time I would have to navigate the Cave of Darkness grew in my stomach; I was in a near panic three-quarters of the way down.

"Panic will do nothing but wear you out even more. Stay calm, stay calm," I mumbled to myself. When I was little, my mother hummed to me in order to take my mind off my panic attacks.

The song "This Little Light of Mine" was all that came to mind. Putting some soul into it, I bobbed and dipped my head to the beat. My anxiety slowly melted away until something small, black, and furry flew into my face obscuring my view.

"Oh! Agh!!!" Frantically I slapped my face battling the tiny creature. The being relentlessly flew into my face over and over like a bird running into a glass window. Drawing my hand into a fist I swung with all my might, connecting with the winged creature. The force of the swing caused me to lose my footing sending me sprawling down several steps, but I somehow manage to stay on my feet. That little tirade almost took me over the ledge of the stairwell.

"Lord God, please protect me from another one of those little things. I may just have a heart attack," I half joked as I rested my hand over my chest.

The lighting from above had all but vanished, the tiny sliver of light no longer enough to ease my mind. My thoughts drifted to the Mezirot. *Should I try it out to examine my surroundings?* Deciding it was best not to draw attention to myself, I kept it in my pocket.

I wondered how Mark survived alone in complete darkness the last few weeks, slowly being driven mad. Mark—his sweet face wormed its way into my mind.

"I'm coming for you," I whispered, hoping my positive vibes would somehow find their way to bring him comfort.

When I finally reached the bottom of the gorge, I missed the last step and twisted my ankle. Tears sprang to my eyes. *Great!* On top of being exhausted, beaten, and scared beyond belief I would now have to limp along at a sluggish pace.

My entire body shook as total darkness enveloped me. I had no idea which way to go. Fingering the material of the Mezirot in my pocket I pulled it out and gasped at the strange phenomenon. The once cool material warmed in my hand as it shone a brilliant blue light against the rocky chasm.

The light revealed a sizable perimeter around me. Deliberately, I spun in a circle taking in my surroundings. The glossy stone walls were forever frozen in black-and-beige striped waves, and a copious amount of condensation created a pleasant glittery effect.

Just before I came full circle, a cloud of navy-blue sparkling dust spiraled before me. The tornadic cloud spun leisurely holding me in my place memorized by its fierce beauty. My breath left my mouth in rapid puffy clouds, my body shook in anticipation.

Several seconds passed then the dust settled, leaving me disappointed, until I discovered what the dust had been trying to hide. The mouth of the

Cave of Darkness materialized, leaving me dumbfounded.

Holding the Mezirot in front of me, I took in the colossal twin gargoyles framing the mouth of the cave. The demonic creatures' predatory gaze sent a chill down my spine. The smooth, shiny, onyx structures were incredible works of art. Blood-red rubies shone from the eye sockets looking much like large red moons. The glow of the Mezirot illuminated the gems, casting a crimson hue over my body.

Impulsively, I walked to one of the structures and ran my hand along the smooth stone. The intricate details of the stone feathers felt so delicate, so real. *How did these works of art end up down here?* I wondered.

Shaking my head, I peered into the mouth of the cave. If I had any doubt before of being in the right spot, I no longer did when I peered inside. Darkness guarded the cave, screening me from even the tiniest of glimpses inside. The light of the Mezirot flickered as I approached the opening. I knew its power would wane once inside. Limping on my now-throbbing ankle, I hobbled through the mouth of the cave.

Chapter Fourteen

The Cave of Darkness

The second my foot crossed the threshold, my vision became highly limited, making the journey painstakingly slow. The first area I wandered into was a circular room surrounded by five tunnels all leading in different directions.

There was no real reason I picked the first tunnel, other than it was closest to me. A few moments later it abruptly stopped in a dead end. Frustrated, I exited the area and shuffled to the next tunnel over.

To my relief, the passageway wasn't a dead end but a narrow winding path. The rock walls were adorned with deep gouges as if someone or something had run its claws along it. Fear rattled my soul, thinking of who or what created those marks.

Lightly I ran my fingertips along the grooves and continued to move. Suddenly without warning my legs fell out from under my body. A scream ripped from my chest. Flailing my arms in circular motions trying to grasp anything but air, I snagged the edge of the ground by my fingertips.

Somehow, I managed to keep the Mezirot in my hand as I hung from the ledge. Hysterical, crazed sobbing rang through the tunnel. It took a full minute to realize the cries were coming from me.

Clumsily I pulled myself back onto solid ground. Sucking air through my teeth and trying not to cry from sheer fear, I sat down to take a few calming breaths. A large rip in my training suit revealed a hulking scrape where a majority of skin from my left side was missing. Between my twisted ankle, the missing skin, and a swollen face, I had little unbeaten flesh left. Sadly, half of my injuries came from my own clumsiness.

Oddly I didn't feel as much pain as I thought I should. Holding the Mezirot in front of me, I assessed my situation. The pit I had almost fallen victim to was too wide for me to cross. *Maybe if I had a grapple hook or could shoot webs from my wrists I could swing from one side to the other. But, not today...not today.* Keeping a better eye on the ground, I backtracked to the main corridor to try another tunnel.

The third tunnel was a bit more successful; however, I had already used half of my time in the first two. Panic kicked in. *Time...time...I am running out of time!* Frantically, I shuffled through the tunnel, my ankle rolling out from under me with each wobbly step I took. With total disregard to anything that might be living in the dark, I cried out for Mark.

"Mark! I'm here..." my voice echoing back was my only reply.

The deeper I traveled in the tunnel, the more disheartened I became. Tons of tiny passages fed off the one I traveled through. The air grew thick as I struggled to pull in a deep breath; my palms grew clammy. There was no way I would have time to explore much longer. The Mezirot's light faded, confirming my fear.

Any hope of finding Mark dimmed with the light. The Mezirot flickered. The tiny teal beam pulsed like a strobe light. I had gone too far. There was no way I would make it out of the cave in time. To make matters more grim, the tunnel dead-ended just as the one I traveled before. But, in between flashes, something caught my eye.

At first glance, the object looked to be an odd-shaped rock. I took two cautious steps closer. *Could it be?*

"Mark?" I crept towards the figure, squinting my eyes. "Is that you?"

The Mezirot flashed off, on, off, on. The figure craned his neck in my direction. *Something is wrong. Is he hurt?* The flashing was too rapid. I couldn't make out what was going on. He crawled towards me like a bear, the light off, on, off. Off. No light.

I shook the Mezirot, a feeble attempt to get some residual juices flowing. The scuffling of feet on the ground made my skin crawl. The light came back on momentarily and I saw that Mark was just a few feet away now, with his mannerisms mimicking that of a wild animal. He sniffed the air, taking in my scent, a growl rumbling in his throat.

My brain figured it all out too late. *Too late!* Mark was gone. His face was distorted, crazed. His normally beautiful blue eyes were bloodshot, the clear blue now a dull gray. His jaw fell limply to one side as foam dripped from the corner of his mouth, his pale skin soaking in the blue light of the Mezirot.

The Mezirot flashed once again. He was rising to his feet. The light continued to flash much more slowly now. Off…. On…. Off….

With each flash of the light Mark took a step towards me. My legs were frozen in fear. The boy wasn't sane. If he caught me, I would die. *Why won't my legs move?*

"God, please let him recognize me. Please don't let him kill me," I begged.

Mark licked his lips and growled again. His once droopy mouth curled into a wicked smile covering half of his face. Then in the flicker of the Mezirot, his face filled with disgust; hate ruled him now.

He didn't know me. I turned to run and the power of the Mezirot flickered out for good. We were now encompassed in complete, utter, and total darkness. Quickly, I understood the fiend's fears. My eyes saw nothing. Reaching my hand out to touch the rough stone wall, I used it as a guide to navigate through the tunnel. Half limping half running, I stumbled through the cave, hearing Mark's hungry cries close behind me.

Chapter Fifteen

Marcus: Until Sunrise 1891

Satan had given him until sunrise. Marcus wanted to take advantage of every free moment. He left the swinging tree, deciding he wouldn't taint that special place for his father. It was their place, and he wanted his father to have only fond memories of the beloved tree.

The woods might be a good place. He rarely visited the retched place since he and Emma imagined up the ghost of old Mr. Smith who had owned the land just before his family bought it.

It was Emma who thought up the ghost, but as usual when his twin came up with some scheme he was right there alongside her.

Emma had imagined that Mr. Smith was a warlock who spent his time hunting small unsuspecting children and stealing their souls while they slept comfortably in their warm little beds. She had imagined he waited in the woods by day, stalking his prey, studying their every move.

He and Emma both went a fortnight without a wink of sleep for fear of Mr. Smith dragging their souls from their bodies. He chuckled at the thought of the whipping they received when their momma found out why they both refused to leave the house. She chastised them something awful for creating stories about a great Christian man such as Mr. Smith.

There was no beating known to man that would remove the frightful images of Mr. Smith from their mind. Nor did it matter how many times their parents explained that Mr. Smith was a kind man who died of old age, Marcus could never shake the fear of what he and Emma conjured up.

Even now as he stepped a foot into the tree line, he felt a shiver run down his back.

A slight breeze rustled the branches above his head and a dense fog billowed at his feet. It was too much; he backed out of the tree line. The woods wouldn't become his final resting place. Shaking his head, he realized the sun would soon rise.

Torn between finding a place where his family wouldn't find him and not having his body defiled by the creatures of the farm, he chose closer to home. It would be a small comfort to gaze upon his childhood home as his life leaked from his body.

The barn gave him a view of his home and the swinging tree. He knew he would be found quickly. The happiness that surrounded his home would soon be shattered. While his parents experienced the miracle of Emma's healing, they would endure the loss of their son. In the horizon, the sky started to change from black to a glorious pink. It was time. He skulked away from the back of the barn and looked at his home.

Marcus placed the barrel of the shotgun to his chin, his thumb on the trigger ready to pull at his brain's command.

"God, please forgive me for what I'm about to do," he whispered to the sky.

Chapter Sixteen

Only One Way Out

A trickle of blood ran down my chin as I bit my lip to stifle a scream. My leg throbbed from damage sustained after hitting a large rock jutting from the wall. Something warm and wet profusely ran down my leg. Not caring if my leg fell off, I wouldn't stop. Death would occur if I stopped.

Mark's blood-thirsty grunts fueled my fear, driving me forward. Pain or not, I sprinted, running my hands along the rocky wall. I prayed that if my life ended abruptly, it would happen at the bottom of a rocky pit rather than what Mark's sickened mind had planned. A distinct thump resounded, and Mark's garbled cries caused me to pause. Turning back was stupid. I had to keep moving. However, it was Mark—

"Ray…Ray…Help me…if you can hear me, I need your help," I cried into my mind.

"For the love of all that's evil, child! What mess have you gotten yourself into now?" Ray sounded exasperated.

"Mark has changed, I'm too late. The Mezirot is dead…Ray, he is…something very dark." I had to stop. I couldn't feel my way around and talk with Ray. Pressing my body against the wall I stood motionless listening for Mark.

"Oh, for the love of…didn't I say something bad would happen?" Ray asked testily, then plowed on. "That creature isn't Mark, it's a decoy. The Dark One knew you would come for him. He planted a shape-shifting fiend in the Cave of Darkness disguised as Mark. The fiend is…crazy…dangerous-hungry. If it catches you…" Ray's words trailed off.

I had a pretty good idea what may happen to me if I were caught. As quick as fiends were, I was surprised I hadn't been captured or eaten right off.

Sitting still would be signing my death warrant; stumbling and faltering, I moved on. Blood caked my legs and started to dry, and my skin crackled like ice in warm water. Shooting pain followed a never-ending loop through my calves.

If only Ray hadn't thought to mix the transporter serum with Satan's blood, my soul wouldn't have the ability to feel physical pain in Hell. It would have been quite nice to not feel anything, as every surface of my body throbbed with pain.

"Put the Mezirot in your pocket. It may recharge enough to give you a few more minutes of light."

"Ray, why didn't you tell me that before?" Hurriedly I stashed the scrap of fabric in my pocket.

"Just move," Ray grumbled.

"You picked the wrong girl to do these experiments on," I whimpered, scraping away tears that leaked from my eyes.

"I didn't make a mistake." Ray left my mind. At first, I didn't understand what happened to our connection. But a few minutes into my plight and another voice cut into my mind.

"Meadow." A female's voice, I said nothing. "Meadow…I know you hear me."

"What is the point of this, Beth?" I snapped, confused by why I was there. "I cannot win. I'm not strong enough or smart enough or brave enough. I called to God, but He doesn't answer."

"All of those things are lies…the seed of doubt…of loneliness. Satan knows how to attack us by planting doubt in our minds, by making us feel like God isn't there, that He doesn't care. It gives Satan power over us when we believe those lies."

"But I…"

"Of course, *you* aren't strong enough, but *God is!* Do you think God would allow you to make it this far to die? And if it's your time to go, He's going to take you—no matter where you are—to a place more amazing than you could imagine. But for the sake of all of us who care for you, don't give up. Fight! You have to learn to let God do what He does." Beth's words sunk in, but I wasn't ready to hear the truth. "I can't do this anymore. There is no way I can save Mark. I can't even save myself."

"Ray said he asked you to put the Mezirot in your pocket to recharge it. Did you do that?"

"Yeah," I answered.

"You will only have about ten minutes to get out of the cave once you expose it to the darkness again. The Mezirot needs exposure to our world to fully charge or at the very least it needs a break from the curses that plague the cave. Use your time wisely. Ray confirmed that the Cave of Darkness and the area around it are protected against transporting. It's Satan's way of keeping the fiends from escaping when they have been banished. You will have to get somewhere safe and transport back to us."

"I can't leave without Mark."

"I'm going to be honest with you. You don't have much time left. The change has begun, your body here has already turned red. If you could see well in the cave, I'm sure you would notice it there as well."

"I think I feel it, but if it goes much further I will come home, I promise. Right now, I have to do all I can to save Mark."

"Be careful and come back as soon as you can. The Mezirot should have some power now. Try it and move quick. I will see you soon."

"Yeah...soon."

And with that I was alone again. Thrusting my hand in my pocket, I gripped the Mezirot tightly in an attempt to squeeze any bit of light I could from the tiny scrap. The light was faint, but I could still see about six inches in front of me. That speck of light was my only hope of getting out of the cave.

Not to waste time, I took off in the direction I thought to be the mouth of the cave. There are two words to explain what happened next—directionally challenged. Three times I navigated the tunnels like a pro—left, right, left, right, then right only to find myself at a dead end. At the start of my fourth attempt, the Mezirot once again flickered out, this time without the dramatic strobe effect. It just died.

Peeved, I jammed the Mezirot in my pocket again in hopes of a recharge. Fear crushed my chest. Time would run out before I could escape. All hope was lost of making it out alive. And worse yet, the change was consuming my body while the blackness of Hell seduced the dark corners of my mind.

Chapter Seventeen

A Deal

Nancy watched Ray from afar, wondering how he would receive her presence. She knew he would be angry with her for how she handled things with Meadow, but he would get over it eventually. After all, they would have eternity to work through past transgressions.

"Hello, Father."

"Ah Nancy, I was wondering when you would drop in to see your old pa." Ray turned to see his daughter, a plastic smile painted across his face.

She gasped at his appearance. Ray's once perfectly tanned skin was now a brilliant red, his eyes solid black. Even the tufts of white hair sticking off either side of his head surprised her. Back in the day, he was a handsome man who was well kept and impeccably dressed. Her nose drew up in disgust at the dirty robe that hung loosely from his thin frame.

"The Dark Lord has shunned me. I have no one to turn to," Nancy whined.

"I see…and you thought after that stunt you pulled running away with my transporter I would forgive you so easily? Well you're mistaken."

"What if I can catch her? I'm told she's here. We could deliver her to the Dark One, then he will no longer be upset with me," Nancy groveled.

"Hmmm…" Ray rubbed his chin in mock concentration. "Nah, I think I'll pass but thank you for the offer. Now leave," Ray said with a finality Nancy recognized from childhood. There would be no changing his mind unless she had something of value in exchange.

"When I get in his good graces, I'll tell him you helped Meadow. He'll end you," she shot over her shoulder.

Ray chuckled. "Go ahead, child. The thought of eternity is rather daunting, especially in present company."

"I will get her myself," Nancy spun on her heels, stomping off to implement Plan B.

*　　　*　　　*

As well as I could guess, twenty minutes had gone by and I tried the Mezirot again to see if it would give me light. The parchment glowed for two seconds then puttered out. I had depleted its power.

The darkness pulled at my deepest, darkest thoughts and dangled them in my mind. Feelings of hate for the Geeks, my parents, and myself raged through my entire being. My anger grew, thinking of how cozy and sweet it must be to be sitting in the Geeks' lair without a care in the world while I rotted in Satan's dwelling. If I could get my hands on them—I heard something.

Tilting my head sideways I waited, holding my breath. An ever-so-slight hissing sound filled my ears. *What iss it? A voice*...a human voice, followed by the hissing grating noise I associated with the fiends. The human voice was female and heartbreakingly familiar.

"We have to find her," the woman whispered urgently.

The fiend cackled. "Oh, we'll find her alright. She's a sitting duck."

Pressing my body against the rocky wall, I froze in place. A red light rounded the bend of the tunnel. Someone's presence filled my mind. *Strange, I can feel that now.*

"Kid, they're coming for you," Ray said. "Apparently you roughed up a few fiends which your mother found at the bottom of the gorge. Their bodies tipped her off to your whereabouts."

"It's too late. They're here. There's nowhere to run, plus they have lighting, good lighting by the looks of things."

"Interesting...your mother has made some powerful friends rather quickly..."

"What do I do, Ray?"

"Get caught. I can't help you right now, but she's your mother. Play the victim. Her plan is to deliver you to the Dark One herself, so she can gain favor with him. He wasn't happy with her performance when she was on

Earth."

Ray continued, "She won't take you straightaway. She has no idea what is going on in the real world–she will question you before she hands you over. I'm sure she desires information about your father and the old Gander crew."

"If I let them take me, I may run out of time and not be able to leave."

"As long as you have the Mezirot, you should be okay. It may not light up any longer, but you will find that there are certain useful properties available to you when you're in need. Your friends on earth are prepared to use extreme measures to keep your body alive if necessary."

"Extreme measures?"

"Don't ask, kid."

Huffing in protest I realized it didn't matter how they did what they did if they kept me alive. I needed more time, and they were going to give that to me.

"Okay, I'm going to call for her now," I said, my lower lip trembling. I wasn't ready to face my mother, her deception literally made me cringe.

"Be strong, child. You're a fighter; you will make it." I shook my head at Ray's kindness. The man went from hot to cold in two seconds.

Taking in a few deep breaths to compose myself I thought of my mother. As a child I feared the dark and she was there to chase away the scary monsters I created in my imagination. When upset or frustrated, she was there to build me up. And here she was once again, in my darkest hour. Unfortunately, this time she had no interest in protecting me from the boogeyman. Now she *was* the boogeyman.

"Help," my voice barely squeaked above a whisper. I cleared my throat and tried again. "Is someone there? I need help!" My voice bounced off the rocky walls. Limping towards the light, my shoulders hunched in defeat, I heard a harsh whisper.

"Shhh, did you hear that?" my mother asked.

"Yes, it came from over there," the raspy voice of a fiend answered.

The shuffling of feet grew louder. The hot burning lava of fear bubbled inside my stomach. I could handle my mother but where there was a fiend, there was a fight. I curled my hands into fists.

"Ye..yes I'm here, please help," I croaked.

"Oh, Meadow, there you are! I have been so worried about you." My mother ran around the corner and folded me into her arms. I grimaced when she squeezed my raw, bruised body.

"What are you doing here?" I asked, pulling away from her, my eyes drinking in her reaction. A fantastic actor, her eyes brimmed with tears and filled with joy at the sight of me.

"Shh…Later. We'll talk later. The light only lasts so long down here. We have to get you to safety before the Dark One finds us." How sweet she was to think of my safety.

Looking at the fiend I was surprised to see he held a glass orb in his hands. The orb, not much larger than a marble, splashed a dull red light against the walls of the cave. I cut my eyes back to my mother. She was examining me.

Her body stiffened, as if she could sense something had shifted, that I was different. She placed her hand firmly on my shoulder and led the way out of the cave. I didn't fight her but followed willingly; it was the only way.

Three minutes…three minutes is all it took to make it to the mouth of the cave. Disappointment flooded my soul; I had been so close. My mother wrapped her hand around my upper arm and squeezed tightly, preventing me from fleeing. She need not worry about that. I was so banged up, I wouldn't dare try to escape. It was as if my strength fled my soul when the Mezirot lost its power.

Instead of taking me up the stone staircase leading to the landing, we hooked a right and continued along the shadows until we approached a cavern. My mother pushed me inside, the fiend followed us closely. Once inside, the fiend ran his fingers in the air at the cavern's opening, and a green force field appeared.

"What's that?" I asked, perplexed.

"It's to keep you in mostly. That barrier will prevent you from transporting out. It also makes this area soundproof, so no one will hear us," my mother answered. "Have a seat." She pointed past me into the room.

I warily glanced around the cavern. Several chairs carved from what my father used to call fool's gold surrounded a flat-top boulder that functioned as a table. As far as rock furniture went, I suppose it was nice—kind of upper-class cave-mannish.

Perched on the nearest chair, I studied my surroundings. There wasn't much to look at besides our shadows dancing across the stone walls from the light of the wall torches.

"When are you turning me over?" I glared at my mother. It was important she knew I had hardened my heart against her. Of course, deep down I still loved her; she was my mother after all.

Conjuring up feelings of hate nearly killed me, especially when she looked as she always had. Beautiful, young, her eyes filled with love and compassion. The only thing amiss was that her normally frosted hair was a dark matted mass and her clothing was dirty and torn. Upon closer inspection, she did have slightly pink skin and a yellow glow around her eyes like the fiends of Hell, but otherwise she was—Mom.

Where is the evil woman who tried to kill me days before? Where is the woman who helped Ray perform those hideous experiments? I didn't see her. All I saw was my mother. The gentle woman who held me close at night, who read me fairy tales when I was a child, who taught me all I knew.

"I haven't decided." She wrung her hands, looking me over. She wasn't sure how she would be received by Satan and his crew.

"Let me know when you decide." I leaned back, placed my hands on the back of my head, and kicked my heels up on her table, something she would never allow at home.

"How dare...you have certainly changed your attitude, and not for the better I might add!" She scrunched up her eyes and stared at me.

"I suppose that would have something to do with having a murderer for a father and a demon mother. Things like that really change a person." I spoke to her as if she were dim, trying to get a rise out of her, but it didn't work.

"Murderer?" She raised her brow in disbelief.

"Yes, your sweet husband killed Hugo Romano," I spat at her, the tremble in my voice betraying my courage. My eyes stung with tears. *Don't cry in front of her,* I chanted in my mind.

"How unfortunate; however, Hugo should have never turned his back on us. We won't fail in our mission to the Dark One."

"You have already failed," I murmured.

My mother's head snapped as if slapped. "Do you think you will defeat me? You're stuck here. It won't be long before you're just like the rest of us."

"Not going to happen." I jumped to my feet, shoving my face inches from hers. She backed up, her eyes widened. I could use her fear to my advantage. She needed to know she had no power over me, not anymore.

"We shall see," she said, placing a hand over her chest, her nostrils flaring—a sure sign she was angry.

"We shall," I taunted, turning on my heels. Choosing the farthest wall from her, I leaned against it, shooting what I hoped was a menacing glare in her direction.

The fiend kept its eyes on me as it stood next to my mother.

"What?" I shouted at the creature, allowing my anger to get the best of me.

"Don't start with me, child. I will tear the flesh from your bones with my teeth, and trust me, I will take my time doing it."

I gulped and looked away from the monster. It was best I didn't get in a tussle with the fiend, I was too weak. Every muscle fiber in my body cried with exhaustion.

Then he turned to my mother and said, "You need to find Ray and let him know you have the girl. Maybe now you have bargaining power."

My mother looked at me. "Has Ray contacted you?"

I shrugged my shoulders, something she hated. My defiance infuriated her but there wasn't much she could do to force me into submission. As a matter of fact, based on her behavior, if I played my cards right, I could have the upper hand and overtake her quickly. I just needed to get the fiend out of the picture.

However, the fiend ruined my plans by whispering to my mother, "Give her some space and time to cool off. Go find Ray. See if he has reconsidered. I will watch her while you're away."

"She's been training. She may overtake you. We will never gain favor with our master if she—"

The fiend broke through her words, a smirk covering its face. "She has trained for all of a week. Do you think she can beat me? The girl is weak. I can feel her strength leaving her soul. The time her training would do her any good has past." The fiend looked at me hungrily.

He was right. I could literally feel my energy fleeing my soul at an alarming rate. My mother eyed me as well. Satisfied with what she saw, she agreed to go.

"Okay, I won't be long. If she tries to escape..." she eyed me for a moment. "...kill her."

My mouth dropped open, but she didn't pay any attention as she disappeared through the green barrier that held me prisoner.

Once my mother departed, I walked back to the dull gold chair and slumped into it. The fiend continued watching me silently. After several minutes, he sat opposite of me. I desired to kick his sharp pointy teeth straight down his ugly throat. Instead I stared deep into his overly large black eyes daring him to say something.

He wasn't scared of me and he had no reason to be. Being stuck in Hell for so long had stripped me of all I had, and my head drooped slightly. Holding myself upright was a chore. Time was running out. I knew I was going to die or change into one of them soon. I prayed the Geeks could sustain my body on the other side.

"I can free you from this place," the ugly creature spoke, the words gargling from his throat. His snake-like tongue flickered out of his mouth, wrapping around his sickeningly sharp teeth before shooting back into his filthy mouth.

"Why would you?" I asked, eyeing the razor blades that tipped the creature's fingers. My heart did a skip beat as I realized this being could rip me to shreds if he chose to.

"You have something I... need. Not to mention Satan won't win. He never does in the end," he answered.

"What do you mean?"

The fiend tilted his head. "God wins, doesn't He? Does He not always prevail?"

"Yes?" I said unsure of the real answer.

'Why do you doubt?'

The words filled my ears, yet I'm certain only I heard them. *God is that you? Why do I doubt? I'm sorry, God...I fail You in my heart...in my mind.*

The fiend continued, "Allow me to help you. All I desire is to live in peace and roam freely among my own. I may be no more than a filthy creature to you, but the Fire Cave is my home. I have been abhorred as has your mother, but if I give my master something he desires, I may win back his favor."

I believed the creature, but I needed a reason to help my enemy. "Even if what you say is true why would I help you?"

"I'm all you have; the change is taking place rapidly. Either you trust me or stay here for eternity." The fiend folded his wrinkled fingers together. He had a point, somewhat.

Closing my eyes, I willed my mind to connect with Ray's, but silence filled my brain. It was as if he were blocking me out. I had to make a choice.

"What do you want in exchange?" I leaned forward, resting my elbows onto the stone table.

"The Mezirot."

"No way! I need it!"

"The Mezirot or you can stay here and rot. The boy will suffer, and you will be stuck here for—"

"How?" I interrupted.

"Pardon?" The monster seemed perturbed that I interrupted his gloom-and-doom speech.

"How will you help me with Mark?"

"I will subdue him and get you to a point where you can transport yourself back to where you belong."

"Once Mark and I are safe, and somewhere we can transport from, I will give you the Mezirot." Extending my hand to shake, I waited for his reply.

The fiend pondered my words for a moment, then smiled at me. He gripped my hand tightly, his disgusting yellow nails digging into my skin. I cried out in pain and pulled back. It hadn't broken the skin, but thin half-moon indentations were on the top of my hand.

"Let me see it," he said ignoring my cries.

Leaning back, I thrust my hand inside my pocket and pulled out the Mezirot. Gripping it tightly to prevent the demon from snagging it away, I lifted it into the air. Brilliant light burst from the fabric. The fiend and I concealed our eyes to protect them from the brilliant glow. If only the Mezirot were anywhere near that dazzling in the Cave of Darkness.

"Must have charged a bit."

"What?" The monster asked confused.

"Nothing," I mumbled still in awe of the Mezirot's bright light.

Not only was the light bright, but the Mezirot surged strength through my soul. Electric energy flowed through my veins. The red that had taken over my skin paled, the effects of the change reversing.

Quickly, I shoved the Mezirot back into my pocket. The fiend couldn't know about its healing power. Setting my face in a downcast scowl, I tried my hardest to look weak and miserable. It took all within me not to smile at the power I discovered in that miraculous, frayed scrap.

Ray told me the Mezirot was more powerful than he had time to explain; what other powers did this tiny object hold? My stomach knotted at the thought of handing over such a potent item to a fiend. But I had a choice—the Mezirot or Mark—it had to be Mark.

"We must go now if we are to save Marcus before Nancy returns."

"Where is he?" I asked.

The fiend tilted his head to the side and tapped his temple with his index finger. "Why, what do you mean? Did you not see the boy in the Cave of Darkness just moments ago?" He asked smugly. He knew; he knew I had information and by the look on his face he knew who had fed me said information.

"I...I think I'm being tricked... Mark is... he is hidden somewhere else." I stumbled through my blunder.

"Well, now I know where you get your information. Our master planted a lie to see if Ray would betray him. He suspected Ray had a soft spot for you."

Rage filled my body. I didn't know what to do or who to trust. My strength was back. I could try and take the fiend down and run. My eyes darted to the only exit, and my heart dropped. The green force field was still there. Even if I overcame the fiend, there was no way out.

"Don't try it or I will kill you," the fiend read my thoughts.

"Leave Ray out of this," I deflected. The fiend snickered, knowing he had me in a tough spot, but he let it go.

"Don't worry. I rather like Ray. I will keep his secret for now, but remember if you cross me, I will have him taken care of. And to answer your question, Marcus is still down there. I have never seen anything look as he does. If I were you, I would have left when I had the chance. If you give me the Mezirot, I will let you go free right now, no one has to know you abandoned him."

"Wait. You have been abhorred by Satan. How would you know

anything about Ray or Satan or Mark?"

"Satan sends my brothers around to keep an eye on me, to make sure I'm not planning an uprising with the others who have been shunned. My brothers are incredibly dumb and share more than they should." The demon forced the words through his clenched jaw.

From my experience with fiends, that sounded about right. I nodded my head. As much as I hated it, I had to trust the monster. The fiend could be leading me to my death, or he could be helping me. Mark may be in the cave, or he could be kept under the watchful eye of Satan and his fiends. Ray may or may not be helping me, but I had only one way out of my prison, and it was with this fiend.

The monster walked over to the doorway and gently ran his index finger down the barrier which melted away momentarily, then reappeared as a deep blood red.

"That will keep her out for a while," the fiend said admiring his handy work.

"What is it?"

"Another barrier. It conceals this room from plain sight. She will have a hard time finding this place again," he smirked.

"What will my mother do to you?" I asked.

"She has no power here," the fiend snarled. "She should know better than to trust a fiend. We're taught to serve only the Dark One."

His words scared me. *Isn't that what I'm doing? Trusting a fiend?*

"It sounds like you're serving yourself," I said bluntly.

He chuckled. "Yes, yes, it looks that way but, in the end, I'm doing what is best for my master. He needs me. Most of my brothers have very little sense. I'm one of the few who can think coherently." It was sad the dependency these fiends felt for Satan. They clung to him as if he were their last hope.

"We must hurry," the creature said standing up.

The fiend crouched down and pushed the stone table against the wall with all his might. Hidden underneath the round slab was a tunnel leading underground.

"What's this?" I asked, apprehensive about where the demon would lead me.

"Shortcut," he answered distractedly, leading me down a tight trail. The fiend's lanky body contorted–he dropped to all fours–maneuvering through the tight tunnel. His shoulder blades nearly popped out of his skin to fit in the tunnel.

For once I was thankful for my short stature. The shaft weaved from side to side and then steeply climbed up. Torches lit the way until we stepped out onto a narrow ledge about a fourth of the way up the gorge. We climbed up an incline just to shimmy down a much narrower ledge. The heels of my feet were the only part of my body touching solid ground. I moved slowly, deliberately, with my back against the wall.

Our travels—although painstakingly slow—were going well until a piece of the ledge crumbled under my feet. A scream flew from my mouth as I plummeted to the ground several yards below. Pain wracked my body, as I lay there on my back trying to make the world right itself again.

Blinking back tears of pain, my body shook where I lay. Stealthily, the fiend climbed down and pulled me to my feet. I turned my head so the fiend couldn't see the tears leaking from my eyes.

Surprise overcame the pain as I wondered why the fiend didn't take advantage of my injury to snag the Mezirot and run. He easily could have. I said nothing but continued to follow the monster limping along. I badly wanted to reach inside my pocket and let the Mezirot heal me, but I waited. If the beast knew the power that little piece of fabric held, he may not take kindly to me holding on to it any longer.

We continued our trek down the winding path until once again I found myself staring into the mouth of the Cave of Darkness. I shuddered, thinking about the Mark I saw before and part of me wanted to leave him in the cave. Returning to Cassy and the Geeks sounded like a good idea. But I could never abandon him; he didn't deserve to be in Hell.

"When we save Mark, you will help me keep him restrained until I transport?"

The fiend looked at me if he were about to refuse. "I said I would help you." It bowed its head to me, gesturing to the cave entrance.

"After you, Meadow Fields," he said in the grating voice that was prevalent with the fiends and always managed to set my teeth on edge.

Taking a step forward I pulled the Mezirot out of my pocket and held it firmly in my hands. Enough time had passed that the old piece of parchment had recharged somewhat but the lighting was worse than it had been before.

"Why can't you use your light ball...thingy you had earlier?" I asked.

"Move!" The fiend's pointy nail shot into my back.

"Hey," I cried out but started moving despite myself.

My fist clutched the Mezirot close to my body, afraid the fiend would snag it from me and run. I still didn't trust the creature. Fear of the fiend overtaking me and abandoning me in the cave bubbled in my stomach.

"Where do we look for Mark?" I asked.

"When Nancy and I were searching for you earlier, we found him in a crater deep enough to hold him captive." The fiend chuckled, and I shot him a nasty look. "His madness will prevent him from thinking clearly enough to escape." The fiend laughed harder. The temptation to punch it upside its head was great, but I abstained.

"You have to lead the way. I don't know where to go," I snapped, waiting for the fool of a fiend to stop laughing. The silly thing reminded me of a hyena.

"Remember our deal, girl," the fiend said growing serious, his tone let me know he didn't trust me. He looked down at my hand, his eyes hungrily drinking in the sight of the Mezirot. "I will kill you if you cross me. Now get going." He shoved me in the back so hard I stumbled forward.

We walked for a short time, the fiend directing me expertly throughout the tunnels. The Mezirot quickly faded. The strength it had given me vanished with the light.

"We're getting closer." The fiend's voice broke through my thoughts.

"My light is running out. We won't make it out of here if we don't find him soon. Do you have the light you used earlier?"

"My fire orb? I save those for special occasions," the fiend grumbled. He was searching the ground.

"A fire orb?" I asked.

"Those of us lucky enough to be favored by the Dark One were gifted with different things. For some, sets of fire orbs, for others, the gift of telepathy or death orbs...there were many. I chose the fire orb in case I found myself in the Cave of Darkness. Now be quiet. I'm looking for the boy," the fiend snapped.

"Sure thing, buddy," I quipped. The fiend shot me a hate-filled and slightly confused look.

Mark's face popped into my mind, and my hands trembled. *What would he be like? When I last laid eyes on him, he was ready to rip me apart. How would we return him to his normal sweet self once I got him back home?*

"Hurry up. If your light runs out we will be stuck in this cave. Believe me when I say you won't like what will happen if we're stuck together here in the dark."

Clenching my teeth, I had to fight the impulse to show the fiend who was boss. I was in no position to fight this fiend. Not as I grew weaker with the fading of the Mezirot.

"See how the ground dips up ahead? He's down there." I walked slowly towards the hole and peered down.

To my relief Mark was there. I cringed when I saw him. If possible, he looked worse than he did the first time I saw him. His dark hair stuck to his sweat-covered face, his pale skin almost translucent. My heart cried out for the boy who sat there in the dark by himself. He was no longer the boy I knew, but I prayed I could make things right for him.

Mark sat crouched on the rocky ground, crocodile tears leaking from his sweet red-rimmed eyes. Going to him now would be a mistake. If he attacked me, I would be a goner. I backed up, bumping into the fiend.

"Well, there he is," he snarled, pushing me away.

"You said you would assist me in getting him to the top of the gorge."

"Give me the Mezirot," the demon demanded, holding his hand towards me expectantly.

"No way. You get it when Mark and I are safe to transport." I refused to budge on that point. If I gave up the Mezirot, Mark and I would be stuck in eternal darkness plagued by our own madness. The fiend would see to that.

"How do I know you will keep your end of the deal?" The fiend looked me up and down.

"Because Mark is more important to me than this piece of garbage." I shook the Mezirot under the monster's nose. "And because I don't plan on coming back so it's of no use to me. You keep a hold of Mark and make sure he is restrained until we make it to a safe transport spot—then we do an even swap. Once you have the Mezirot, I transport back home."

"If you fool me, girl, I will make your grandfather pay." The fiend narrowed his black eyes at me.

"I keep my word, but just so *you* know, I will spend the rest of my life hunting you down if you don't hold up to your end of the deal."

"Ha! Fat chance of you living long enough. Once you take this boy again, the Dark One will come for you. Stupid girl."

And just like that I lost my temper.

The stupid fiend with his sniveling voice and cocky ways had pushed me too far. Before the creature saw it coming, I pounced on his back and put him in a headlock. My fist pounded down upon the beast's head in rapid-fire succession while the fiend squalled like a teen girl.

With a quickness I hadn't yet grown accustomed to, the fiend ran backwards into the rocky wall of the tunnel emptying my lungs of air once again. But I kept my hold on him. The fiend dropped to the ground and rolled from side to side trying to lose me. We struggled on the ground, rolling on top of one another.

At some point I dropped the Mezirot and the fiend wrapped his ugly hands around the beige scrap. Not having the transporter serum in his blood, the room went dark. Enraged, I fought on, blindly.

Drawing my tiny fist back, I whacked the monster's elfin-shaped head, and he slapped me in my neck. Grabbing my throat, I rolled away in pain, unknowingly making my way close to the pit. One quick movement away from the fiend's approaching footsteps, and I rolled into the dark pit, right into the pit—with a bloodthirsty mad man.

The fiend laughed hysterically from up above. Mark grabbed a hold of my legs–he yanked hard–landing me on my back. Crashing down and banging the back of my head against the wall, I cried for help.

"Get down here and help me, you jerk." It was probably not the most eloquent of requests.

From above, the ball of light belonging to the fiend shined brightly down upon me. I guess now was a special occasion. "Nope," was the fiend's amused reply. He would pay for that.

Mark circled me like a wolf trapping its prey.

"Dang it, Mark. Don't make me hurt you," I said, popping up to my feet. Wobbly, I stood ready to defend myself, my brain throbbing against my skull.

Mark growled in reply. It had to be done; he was going to get the ultimate smack down. A warrior scream rumbled from my chest, breaking the calm of the cave. Barreling straight at him, I rammed my shoulder into his, taking us both down.

Mark was relentless, he bit my leg, hard. Closing my eyes tight so as not to witness my own cruelty, I donkey-kicked the boy in the middle of his chest. Clumsily he climbed to his feet and came back at me.

This time I sprinted around him. Running up his back, I sprung off his shoulders into the air, snagging the ledge of the crater. In one fluid motion I swung up onto solid ground, landing before the fiend. *Thank you, mother for putting me in gymnastics all those years.*

A girlish squeal left the fiend's mouth when he read the rage that fumigated from my soul. He took off with me quick on his heels, the thought of him getting away with my Mezirot was inconceivable. The fiend would have a fight on his hands when I caught him. But as it was, he received his own payback of sorts.

At first, I panicked as the light had all but vanished. There was a cry of anger and foot stomping around a bend in the tunnel. I slowed down and realized what happened. Laughing I peered down at the fiend. "Well, well, what do we have here?"

"Shut up, girl, and get me out." The fiend was in a panic, clawing at his face in despair.

"Give me the Mezirot," I demanded, reaching my hand out for the powerful object.

"No!" The creature crossed its arms across its chest, tilting his ugly pointy chin down towards the ground.

"Give it to me or I won't help you. We can both stay here for all I care. I don't have much longer before I change or die. You—on the other hand—have eternity to be stuck down here. By now my mother knows you have betrayed her so she won't help you. She may even tell your precious master—"

"Don't speak of him," the creature cried out, its lower lip jutting in a pout.

"She may even tell your precious master what you've done," I taunted. "Helping me and his favorite to escape, what kind of minion are you?" I taunted.

"Stop it, stop!" the monster cried, growing frantic at the thought of his master discovering his betrayal. "Take it." He tossed the Mezirot at me. "Now get me out of here!"

Stuffing the Mezirot in my pocket I looked down at the fiend. An overwhelming urge to leave the monster down there to die filled my mind.

The fiend's cries of terror tugged at my heart. It wasn't right, even if the thing was an evil demon of Hell. Not to mention I needed help getting Mark out of his prison and onto safe transporting ground.

"Ugh, shut it, will ya? I'm going to help you."

Admiration crossed its disgusting face. Mixed emotions filled my being. It felt good to do the right thing even if it might come back to bite me in the end.

"Are you ready to keep your word this time?" I spoke as if he were a disobedient child.

"No!" He stomped his overly large foot. The fiend had never been shown mercy or kindness before, and his nonexistent heart didn't know how to process it.

"Fine, see you on the flip side, demon breath." I turned to go.

"Wait, don't go. I will...I will keep my word. I promise."

"Good, here." I stretched my hand down to the frightened monster.

Awestruck he grabbed my hand, and I lifted him out. Precious energy was spent pulling his evil hide out of the pit. Together we walked back to where we had left Mark, the fiend sneaking looks in my direction. I smiled and shook my head. He would never understand generosity or kindness.

Mark was sitting Indian-style, banging the back of his head against the rocky wall and blubbering incoherently when we returned. The fiend hopped down and strolled to Mark as if he weren't a homicidal maniac, and chopped him in the side of his neck. Mark's eyes rolled back into his head and he slumped over face first.

"Hey! What the heck?" I asked, ready to jump down the hole and have another wrestling match with the fiend.

"Trust me. It's easier this way. My fire orb will lose its power soon." Looking at the orb I could see the substance in the glass ball begin to wane. "There is no time to fight with this useless sack. Let's go."

The fiend looked up at me and smiled as though proud of himself.

He did have a point. A sigh of irritation escaped my mouth, but I had to agree. Mark would be easier to deal with if he were—not conscious.

The fiend tossed Mark out of the hole as if he were a rag doll. Once out of the pit, he flung Mark's body over his red scaly shoulders. I led the way back to the entrance of the cave with direction from the fiend, the light of the fire orb fluttering off as we exited the cave. I had to utter a prayer of thanks to the Lord for seeing us through with literally no time to spare.

"Meadow, where are you, child? Nancy knows the fiend has helped you and she is coming. All I can say is get out of here, NOW!" The urgency in Ray's voice was very real.

"We have to move...uh, monster..." I didn't know if the fiend had a name.

"I am! You try carrying this kid on your back!"

"My mother knows you have helped me, and she is coming for us. If she catches us I'm done for. My energy is spent." Once again, I felt the effects of the Mezirot leave me.

"How do you know this?"

"I can't..."

"Ah, Ray...well, I know what gift he chose. Okay then, if we can make it just a little way up these stairs I can transport us up to the top. Surely you can make your way home from there?"

"I can," I nodded.

"Let's move. Nancy knows her way around pretty well considering she has been here only a short time."

On sore, trembling legs, I climbed the stairs with a purpose. We were so close to making it back home, we just had to make it.

"This is good, Master's wards have no hold here. Take my hand." The creature extended his free hand to me while tightening his grip around Mark.

I placed my palm against his and within the blink of an eye we were at the top of the gorge. The fiend dropped Mark on his side. A groan escaped his mouth, but he didn't wake up.

"Careful!" I shouted.

"He's fine. Get over it. Now hand over the Mezirot!" The fiend looked down to his outstretched hand.

"Okay." I rummaged around in my pocket to pull out the mysterious object. It glowed lightly at my touch, then flickered out.

Extending my hand, I started to hand the Mezirot to the fiend, then pulled back for a moment.

"Don't play with me, girl." The yellow around the fiend's eyes changed to red.

"You're right. Here!" I extended my arm again to hand the Mezirot to the fiend.

"Stop!" my mother shrieked, barreling from the tunnel of the Fire Cave. I stumbled back in fear.

My eyes moved from the fiend to Mark's still form. "Here," I thrust the Mezirot into the fiend's chest.

Without the Mezirot on my body, my legs trudged through the air as if moving through a pool of honey. Wondering if I could transport Mark and myself back to the Geeks' lair with so little energy, I trudged to his limp form.

Turning half-fiend worked in my mother's favor. She ran at me in warp speed. Knocking me to the ground, she wrapped her hands around my throat.

"Get off me, you crazy woman," I cried, grabbing a handful of her face and pushing her head back.

"Sit still, you wretched child," was her reply. She jerked her head out of my grasp.

Thrashing my body from side to side to bump her off, I wore out quickly. In defeat, I let my hands drop to my side. My mother's eyes opened wide in wicked glee. The whites of her eyes were now a dark muddy gray and the yellow that lined them cast an eerie sheen down her face. I closed my eyes praying for a miracle. I was so close. We had been so close.

"Shhhh...it will be over soon," she sang in a whisper. Wrapping her fingers tighter around my neck she squeezed.

"God save me," I prayed silently.

Keeping my eyes closed I prepared mentally for the end, but my body was having a hard time letting go. Involuntarily, my hands met my mother's. I tried to pry her fingers from my throat.

My gasps for air were futile as my trachea was closed off. Heavy—my arms grew heavier and started to drift back down to the ground. I felt far away from the struggle. Suddenly her weight left me and I thought, *Surely this is the end.*

Fresh air invaded my nostrils, and I opened my eyes wide in confusion. My mother was gone. Sitting up I looked around the cavern. The fiend had grabbed a fistful of my mother's hair and dragged her away.

Clutched in its other fist was the Mezirot. My heart sank, thinking that tiny scrap may be more valuable than I first realized. Pulling my body across the smooth rocky floor to Mark, I laid my hand on his chest and visualized the laboratory. Darkness overtook me.

Chapter Eighteen

Just Like Him

"Owwww," I groaned rubbing my head with my hand. My throat was dry—
the skin lining my esophagus was cracked.

"Meadow? Are you okay?" Evan's voice invaded my ears. I nodded my
head, unable to open my eyes against the bright overhead light.

"Yes," I whispered.

"Oh, thank God. I thought you were going to be like him…" There was
something in his tone that set my nerves on edge.

I shot up into a sitting position. "Like who?" My heart pounded so hard
it was likely to burst from my chest.

Something is wrong.

The room spun when I stood. Shaking my head, I tried to move. The
world spun, I sunk back against my cot. Mentally, I worked through what
had taken place, but it was fuzzy. Evan was sitting on a stool by my side,
moving back and forth, the stool's wheels squeaking.

"Well…he's not…he's wild, Meadow." Squeak, roll, squeak, roll.

"What?" His words didn't make sense. Squeak, roll, squeak, squeak, roll.

"Like a monster…" The squeaking pierced my brain, I wanted to throw
something. Squeak, squeak, roll, roll.

"Evan, sit still," I begged reaching out to touch his leg.

I assumed Evan was talking about Mark. I knew Mark wasn't 'normal'. I
hadn't really expected him to be; however, deep down I hoped he would be
my Mark again once I brought him home.

"Evan tell me! Is it Mark? Where is he?"

"I...uh...."

"Where is he? Where is he?" Grabbing handfuls of my hair, I tugged and cried. "Tell me, Evan. Where is he?"

Rolling off the bed, I struggled to stand upright. Evan grabbed my arm as I took a few wobbly steps towards the door. He pulled me close.

"What are you doing?" I shrieked, jerking away from his grip.

"There are things you need to know Meadow—you need to hear..." He reached out to grab me again, but I snatched my arm away and huffed. "No, listen, Meadow, wait."

Pushing him aside I took off again. *The holding chamber! That's where Dr. Wright would keep him! Yes, the holding chamber.*

In ten seconds flat, I ran out of steam. Evan caught up with me very quickly. My eyes were seeing double. I leaned against the wall and slid down on my backside. I was more out of sorts than I wanted to be.

"Seriously, do you want to kill yourself?" Evan yelled, crouching down next to me. His face drew up and his chest heaved up and down. He frantically searched up and down the hallway for reinforcements.

His insistence on being there annoyed me. "Listen, I'm not your problem. You don't have to babysit me anymore. I don't need you hovering over me because the Geeks think I need a bodyguard. And to be honest, I don't want you around. The time where I felt something for you is gone." Inwardly I cringed at my own words. My lashing out was no more than a reaction of fear. I knew it but refused to apologize.

Evan, if anything, was a man of pride, and I had crossed a line. He clenched his jaw and looked as if he wanted to say something, then decided it wasn't worth it and shook his head. He jumped to his feet and stalked away, leaving me crouching on the ground.

Pride prevented me from calling to him, from saying I was sorry. Bad feelings filled my heart, wanting him to pay for his past mistakes. Eventually, I would need to deal with those feelings, but now wasn't the time.

Straining to stand up, I pulled my body up the wall. My legs were shaky, but I had to see Mark. However, once I reached the holding chamber, my heart began to pound and beads of sweat appeared across my forehead. A squeal pierced my ears, shaking me to my core.

One moment I was swaying on my feet, the next, all the air in my body was being squeezed from my lungs. Cassy—I wrapped my arms tightly around her neck, mostly to steady the spin of the world. We stayed that way for several minutes before she put me back down. Her embrace made me feel calmer, more in control.

"Hey, Cass, you okay?" I asked looking into my friend's eyes.

She nodded her head. "I'm hanging in there." Grief radiated from her entire being.

"I'm sorry I haven't been there for you…I…"

She shook her head, holding up her hands to stop me. "Later. Dad understood what could happen. He took a risk and it…it didn't work out."

She didn't mean what she was saying. Just below the surface resentment brewed within my friend. In that moment she didn't know who deserved her contempt—me, the Geeks, Satan, or all the above—but it would come out soon enough.

"I guess you want to see Mark, huh?"

Scared of what I might find, I wanted to flee the Geeks' lair and take my chances on the outside world, but Mark deserved better.

"I have to." Cassy gave me an odd look at my choice of words. I knew I had to see him. *But, don't I also want to? Hadn't I fought so hard to bring him back here with me?*

"Beth and Dr. Wright are in there right now. They sedated him earlier. He's not the same, Meadow. The Geeks are afraid the damage could be permanent."

Nodding my head in resignation, I looked down at the ground. *Would Mark be stuck the way he was, deep within his own personal hell? Would Satan rain his wrath upon our lives? Was there anything I could do to make a difference in any of it?* Those questions swam through my mind, but no one knew the answers. We were swimming in uncharted waters.

Without another word, I slapped my hand against the print scanner that granted me access to the viewing room and walked into my worst nightmare. Mark's pale drooping face was pitiful, his eyes begged for death. *Where is he, what is happening in the depths of his mind?*

At my approaching footsteps Beth spun around in her chair. When her eyes locked with mine she almost fell off her seat. "What on earth are you doing? You can't be up right now!"

"No, I need to be here…with him." I looked back at Mark. As hard as it was to see him so broken, it was easier to look at him than Beth. She and my mother shared many similar features, although Beth was a bit younger and her eyes more kind. She wisely bit her tongue, shrugged, and spun back to whatever she was working on.

"At least have a seat," she pointed to a chair on her right. Taking her advice, I sat, trying not to give into the dizziness that beckoned me.

Mark was being held in the same chamber as the fiend had been, but the glass tube that prevented the fiend from transporting wouldn't be used for Mark. Thoughts of the dying fiend filled my mind. We had killed it by making it stay. I wondered how much more death we would see. My heart stopped in my chest as I worried that Cassy or Bubba could be next.

The Geeks decorated the chamber to resemble a bedroom with a twin-size bed and bedside table filled with food that remained untouched. Despite their efforts, the chamber still resembled a glass-encased prison cell. Not able to stay put, I stood, and made my way to Mark.

After I took a few wobbly steps further, Mark spotted me. Slowly he stood and crept my way. Recognition lit up his eyes. *Could it be?* Not to tarnish the moment, I tiptoed closer to the glass. Gently his feet slid across the concrete floor—the scraping of his feet echoed through his chamber—closer. A smile spread across my face, my heart warmed as his lips turned into the familiar smile he had given me hundreds of times. Yet—something was wrong.

With lightning speed, Mark ran the last few feet in my direction, slapping his hands against the glass on either side of my head. Pressing his face to the glass he snarled, gnashing his teeth. Banging his head and fists against the glass over and over, a spot of blood grew larger with each slam of his face.

"Oh, God," I cried, falling onto my backside. Closing my eyes, my heart thundered. I couldn't draw in a breath.

"Get her out of here," Beth yelled. A pair of strong arms belonging to Dr. Wright dragged me from the room. My body went limp, I didn't fight him. A dull roar filled my ears. It was then that I allowed myself to be swallowed into the darkness.

*   *   *

"Oh, why?" I cried, remembering my encounter with Mark as soon as I opened my eyes. My head pounded, causing me to flinch in pain.

Looking around, I realized I was in my living chambers. I felt like death. All I wanted to do was go back to sleep, but my stomach rumbled in need of sustenance. *First, I need a shower.* A thick layer of nasty clung to my body and coated my tongue.

The first set of pajamas I saw in my drawer made me smile. It was a grotesque pink two-piece, fleece set with bunnies that were hiding brightly colored Easter eggs in tall tufts of neon grass. *Cassy...again.*

Thirty minutes later, I emerged from my room much cleaner than I had been. My stomach sent another reminder it was running on empty. The clock on my microwave read nine p.m. Strolling to the kitchenette I prayed someone had stocked my mini-fridge.

It wasn't stocked, but someone had brought me a plate wrapped in tin foil loaded with mac and cheese and a bowl filled with several chocolate brownies. Soul food. Without heating the provisions, I shoveled it in and washed it down with a warm can of Coke. Leaving my mess for another day, I made a straight line back to my bed.

Snuggling under my fuzzy purple blanket I dozed off until the voice of an overly angry demon grandfather interrupted my slumber.

"How stupid can you be?" his voice just short of a dull rumble.

"Ray, I know you're my grandfather and all, but please shut it. I'm not in the mood to deal with you."

Ray gasped. "Don't take that tone with me," his voice both shocked and horrified. "It's a good thing there are light years between us because I would wring your scrawny neck, child!"

"Good night, Ray." I tried to close him out by covering my ears but that didn't work. I needed to find out how to block him from my mind.

"You will never be able to save the boy now." Ray spoke the only words that would keep me from succumbing to sleep.

The upper part of my body shot upright. "What do you mean?"

"You gave the bloody Mezirot away! How could you?" Ray's voice trembled.

I had made a mistake. An image of the greedy fiend with the Mezirot in its claws penetrated my mind. *What had I done?*

"It's just a light, Ray...tell me how to make another one and I will get the Geeks right on it. I mean, how hard can—" I started.

"You cannot make another one, you foolish thing," he snarled.

"Why not?"

"It was made from a fragment of an ancient artifact belonging to Jesus Himself. There is no way to duplicate it."

"That scrap of fabric once belonged to Jesus?" my voice raising by twenty decibels. I had given the demon a remnant that Jesus once owned. A wave of nausea rolled over me.

"Yes, ever heard of the woman who was healed by touching a corner of Jesus' robe?"

"Vaguely," I responded. I knew the story.

"Well, she more than touched His robe. She cut a tiny fragment off and passed it down from generation to generation until some of my people located it."

"I didn't...know..."

"Pfff, of course you didn't."

"But you took something that belonged to Jesus, making it a dark object. How could you?"

"I had already picked sides. Jesus hadn't done anything for me, but the Dark One brought me success. He brought me my greatest accomplishment—the transporter."

"Jesus gave His life for you so that you could live an eternity with Him." I stated.

"Save your speeches for someone whose fate you can change. I'm here forever. Your God never knew me for I never allowed Him into my life. I made my choice. What I'm more worried about is the poor choice you made in giving such a powerful object away!"

Weighing my words, I asked a question I was truly afraid to hear the answer to. "What else could the Mezirot do besides make light in the darkness and give me a boost of energy in Hell?"

"For starters, it could have cured Marcus of his madness. Now I'm afraid he will be stuck like that forever."

Tears burned my eyes. *Why couldn't anything work out? Why wasn't God guiding me? Why did Mark have to suffer because I was an incompetent transporter...an incompetent person?*

"Then I... I will have to come back and get it."

"Ha, I would love to see you try. They will be waiting for you to return.

That fiend knew you couldn't save that boy without the Mezirot. He wants to get Marcus out of the way. Fiends only do what benefits the Dark One and themselves."

"I don't care…I don't care anymore. I don't care what Satan has planned, I don't care what his fiends want to do to me, and I don't really care what you, my mom, or the Geeks have planned. My fate has been sealed no matter what. My life isn't my own. This curse you have brought upon me will hover over my head always."

"There are too many people down here who want you dead, girl. Cut your losses and let the boy go, or bring him back and dump him off." Ray truly believed he was being helpful, but his heart was as black as the Cave of Darkness.

"You're cruel," I said sadly. *Why is my family filled with such heartless people?*

"No, I'm honest. It appears to me your life turned upside down once that boy entered the picture."

"My life was one big lie. Mark just exposed it all. If not for him, I would be dead or worse if it were up to my mother. My days were numbered under her care."

"Enough with the dramatics…"

Sucking a breath in I cut through his words, "Dramatics! Are you kidding me?"

"For the record," Ray interrupted quite loudly, "I don't suggest your coming back here. Your mother is beyond angry, and the fiend has several of his underlings guarding the Mezirot. They are ready to take your head off and hand-deliver it to Satan if you show your face here again."

"Yeah? Well, I refuse to leave Mark like this. However, it appears I will need some help."

"Don't ask me. I'm helping you as much as I can. Ask your friends," Ray added defensively.

"None of them can stand the temperature change for more than a few minutes," I mumbled.

"That's not true. There was another who had powers almost equal to your own."

Evan? No, I couldn't ask him to transport. "That's out of the question."

"You don't have a choice if you wish to save Marcus. You can't do this alone."

How could I possibly ask Evan to risk his life for Mark's, especially after how I had treated him?

"I will find another way. I can't ask him to help me."

"I don't see the problem."

"You wouldn't. By the way, the fiend who has the Mezirot knows you have been passing me information. He seems to be keeping that information to himself right now."

"Well, how unfortunate," Ray paused for a moment. "Hmm–I will have to watch myself–I may not be able to talk to you for a while if I'm to keep up this charade."

Feeling the familiar silence buzz inside my head, I knew Ray had left. His telepathy etiquette needed work. There was no use in trying to get any more sleep. I needed to check on Mark anyway.

Once dressed, I made my way back to the holding chamber and watched Mark from afar. He paced back and forth in his prison like a caged animal. One look at him and I could see there was no change to his mental state. I had been out of my mind to think anything different the night before.

Refusing to go near the glass chamber I stood across the room studying his every move. Mrs. Parker, Bubba's mother, walked in and sat in a chair next to me. She didn't speak; her silence was comforting.

"He's a good guy. I can't watch him live like this…like a caged animal. It's not right."

"I know," she answered, her voice soft. She was one of those women who could light up a room with her smile. She was the sweetest person I had ever met; her son was a lot like her.

"The only person who can help me is the last person I want to ask." -

Mrs. Parker worked my words out in her head before she spoke.

"You know every single person in this building would do anything for you, *especially* the person you don't want to ask." Mrs. Parker grabbed my hand in her own giving me a tiny squeeze and continued. "He wouldn't be here if he weren't willing to do what was needed to protect you. Evan wouldn't be here at all if not for his love for you."

"You're right, but I don't want to use him. I mean if something happened to Evan I—"

"You would go on and live your life just as he would want you to, even if that life involves Mark."

Mrs. Parker released my hand to give me a hug, then stood to leave. Just as she started out the door, she stopped and stuck her head back in the room.

"He's hurting. Even if you don't feel the same way, you need to talk to him. We have to finish...what we the Geeks started, and we can't do that if we're fighting amongst ourselves. You're the only one who can fix this mess we adults have created for you—and for that I'm sorry."

Unable to speak, I nodded my head and swiped away the lone tear that fell from my eye. I hated what was happening, but I knew she was right. Evan and I were the only two who could stop this mess. Mrs. Parker left me sitting there lost in my own thoughts.

Feeling his eyes on me, I looked up to see Mark watching me through the glass. He looked sad and confused. A sob broke from my chest, I looked at the boy I had grown to care for. There was no choice.

Finding Evan wasn't hard. He was in the gym lifting weights. He looked as he did when we were dating. A tug at my heart made me realize how much I missed him. But, there was no time to dredge up old feelings now. I was on a mission.

Spotting me in the mirror on the wall, Evan spoke to me but didn't turn around. "What are you doing here?" His voice was cool, a reminder of how much I had hurt him.

"I need to talk to you," I said.

"Come to apologize?" he smirked. Ugh, the boy was full of himself. He really made it hard to feel any sympathy for him.

"Actually, I am. Evan I..." My voice cracked, and I covered my mouth with my hand. Shoot, not the waterworks. I hated crying in front of Evan, but there was no stopping the floodgates. One would think at this point I would be cried out, but apparently my body produced tears by the bucket-load.

Evan mumbled under his breath, dropped the weights, and—before I could stop him— wrapped his arms around me. Hating how perfectly I fit into his embrace, I tried to pull away, but he held me close. I melted into him. My heart needed comfort.

It didn't mean anything anyway. We were just two old friends who needed affection. Tears fell from my eyes uncontrollably and loud hiccupping sobs flowed from my mouth. Glancing at my face in the mirror-lined wall I could see it was red and splotchy.

I struggled to shut down the tears, but still I cried. I cried for Mark, for Mr. Romano, for Ray. I cried for Cassy, Bubba, the Rosses. I cried for Evan. But most of all I cried for myself and how helpless I felt.

It took a while but once I composed myself I pulled away. Wiping my eyes with the back of my hands, I smeared my tears down my face.

"I need your help." Now was the time to be straight with him, no holding back. My heart fluttered at how close he stood to me, his brown eyes soft with a tenderness I hadn't quite experienced before. It hurt knowing he cared for me. *Where was this Evan back when we were dating?*

"You have to go back?" Evan asked.

"Yes, for Mark...I...he, you and I are his only chance. I made a mistake when I handed the Mezirot over to the fiend."

"You need me to go with you?" His brown eyes looked troubled.

"Yes," I answered, ashamed for asking so much of him.

"My parents told me you and I were the only ones who were able to transport successfully. It has been a long time since I have even tried." He took a step back and paced the floor.

"Oh..." His knowledge once again reminded me how much my friends had hidden from me all these years.

An image of Evan being tortured by fiends flashed into my mind, causing me to flee from the room. *What was I thinking?* I couldn't ask my first love, the boy who still loved me, to help save the new boy I may be falling for—especially when we would have to travel to Hell to do it. *He could die. I could die. We all could die!*

Evan caught up with me in seconds, grabbed me by my arm, and stopped me in my tracks.

"You can't run every time something goes wrong, you know? You are wasting time. In the end, you know we have to go. So instead of making me chase you, let's make a plan and do it."

It was his confidence that had drawn me to him when our friendship had blossomed into something more. He just went for everything he wanted, nothing stood in his way. Evan was right; I had to stop running.

"Meet me in the dining hall in the morning before breakfast and we will plan our trip."

Wrapping my arms around his neck I whispered in his ear, "Thank you."

When I pulled back he was smiling, it warmed my heart. There was no one I would rather battle the demons of Hell with than Evan. He was cunning, quick, and strong. Plus, if he were able to transport as quickly and effectively as I was, we might have a fighting chance. But I needed some insight before I could formulate my plan.

Chapter Nineteen

Help

"Ray...I need your help."

"Oh, how wonderful," Ray's condescending tone made my head spin. Reminding myself to keep a cool head, I ignored his attitude.

"How do we get the Mezirot undetected?"

"You don't...As I said before, the Mezirot is heavily guarded."

"There has to be a way," I said, trying to think of what I could do.

"When you find the Mezirot's location, one of you will need to be bait and distract the fiends...draw them away. Then the other needs to snatch the Mezirot, it won't be easy. You need to have a meeting place...get somewhere safe to transport from, assuming you don't get caught or killed."

Ray's normally condescending tone sounded...defeated...his voice dull, emotionless.

"The closest place will be the rock bridge or possibly the Water Cave," he continued. "Don't allow yourselves to be led into one of the side chambers. Stay out in the open as much as possible. These fiends know every nook and cranny of this place, and if you get off the well-beaten path, you will be a goner. Don't get caught...if the fiends don't kill you, Satan will."

"I...I understand. Do you have any idea where the Mezirot might be?" I asked.

"I don't know right now, but I would assume somewhere near the Fire

Cave. That's where the fiends spend most of their time."

"Okay... did the fiend tell Satan you have been helping me?"

"So far no, but he will when it suits him. I'm not worried. Whatever happens, happens. For now, I wish you the best of luck, my grandchild."

"Thank you, Ra...Gramps," my semi-sarcastic gift to him. All I could give was acceptance that he was my family. No matter where he was, or who he was, he was my grandfather. Although it saddened me that he chose the path he had for himself, it felt nice giving him that. I wasn't sure, but I think Ray liked it as well.

"Bye, kid." Once again I felt him leave my mind.

Spacing out, my mind wandered to what life might be like when all this mess was over. Immersed in my own candy-coated thoughts, I didn't hear Cassy walk in. "Meadow, we need to talk."

"Ugh, why don't these doors have locks?" I groaned playfully.

"One might ask why you're so worried about locks when you're planning another trip to Hell."

Darn. Stalling for time I played dumb. "Uh, what? Who said that?"

"Evan said you two are going back to Hell to retrieve the Mezirot." Cassy responded drily, clearly not amused with my behavior.

Thank you, Evan. "Yes," I said, bracing myself for a fight. I could see in Cassy's eyes that she was ready for a throw-down. If she were lucky I may give in to her wishes.

"Are you crazy?"

Grinding my teeth, I tried not to bite back. She was under a great deal of pain. "I have no choice, Cassy. If we don't, Mark will never get better."

"Do you think Mark would want you to do this?" Cassy shot at me, as if she knew what Mark would or wouldn't want.

"I don't know what he wants. Right now, he has the brain capacity of a zombie on steroids."

"Oh, cut the crap, Meadow. Hide behind your sarcasm and pretend you're tough and don't care. Do you have a death wish? Do you want all our sacrifices to be pointless? Bubba and I gave up our lives to protect you, yet you continue to go where we cannot do that. We can't protect you in Hell!"

"Seriously? I had no idea about any of this so whatever part of your life you gave up..." I gaped, trying to grab the words I wanted to say. "...At least you have been trained. At least you knew what to expect. I have gone into every single bit of this blindly. And you have the nerve to chastise me about danger? I HAVE NO CHOICE! Yes, someone can die and likely that person will be me because I have no idea what I'm doing!"

"Who do you—"

"No, I'm not done." *Lord, please take control of my tongue.* "You have no idea what I'm going through. While you sit here safe and snug, I get the crap kicked out of me by demons who want nothing more than to tear my head off and use it as a soccer ball. Satan, have you heard of him? Satan himself has it out for me. This is a problem—my problem."

"Do you think I like having to sit here doing nothing?" Cassy's voice was shrill enough for only dogs to hear at this point.

"Yeah, I do." Really, I didn't, but I wanted to hurt her. For reasons unknown I wanted to hurt them all, to make them feel the pain and confusion I felt. A few weeks ago, I was a normal girl living the good life. Then out of nowhere I had to become this demon fighting—what? What was I? Just a girl fighting a war someone else started, fighting a war I didn't ask for.

Cassy held her hands up to silence me. Her voice grew dangerously calm, causing my arms to break out in goose bumps. "Don't get smart with me, Meadow. We're all stressed but I cannot handle you acting like a complete...jerk to me right now. What you plan on doing is insane. Do you have a death wish?" she repeated, "or do you just want Evan out of the way, so you don't feel guilty about your feelings for Mark?"

The last statement did it. My body shook violently, and I flung myself to my feet. Taking two large steps to stand in front of my friend, my hand swung back ready to send her head reeling, but I thought of Mr. Romano and stopped.

Cassy looked down at my hand, her face going red. She towered over me by a good foot. Lowering my hand I shouted, "Get out! You have no idea what I'm going through or how I feel. Yes, you lost your father, and I'm destroyed inside because of it, but I have lost everything and may still lose my life."

"You haven't lost everything. You're just too blinded by your own pain to see what you do have." Cassy's face relaxed.

"I said, get out." I wasn't ready to make nice. Cassy stiffened her back and left without a word.

Chapter Twenty

Parental Intervention

In the dining hall, Evan sat at a square table built for two. The black bags under his eyes indicated he had slept about as well as I had. The rigidity of his spine also revealed stress he wouldn't admit to having. He didn't need to say anything to me, I got it. Making a trip to Hell wasn't an easy decision, especially when you have the choice to go or not.

"Hi," I said, taking a seat across from him. I lightly touched his arm, my hand lingering longer than I intended it to. He looked down and sighed.

"You okay?" He asked as he turned his bloodshot eyes back to mine.

I snorted lightly. "As good as I can be. Soooo…I have been thinking the best course of action is to share with each other what we know about the caves. Unfortunately, I don't know much about the layout of Hell, and there are literally hundreds of passageways leading to areas I have no desire to visit. According to Ray, our best bet is to stay out in the open, so we don't get cornered or fall to our deaths. We will likely have to make a trip to the Fire Cave."

Evan's head sagged. "I haven't transported in years. The Geeks and my parents didn't like the idea of me being in Hell. The last time I transported was the beginning of my freshman year in high school. I ended up in the bottom of a dark canyon."

"Were you near the Cave of Darkness?" I interrupted. "Did you see an opening with large gargoyle statues, big ruby eyes?" I made circle shapes with my fingers and placed them around my eyes for added effect.

He shook his head. "It was too dark to make anything out. The quiet was unnerving, and I could see ledges snaking their way up the walls."

"Anything else?"

"No, one time I saw a lake but it kind of gave me the creeps, so I transported back pretty quick." He looked down at his hands.

"I know what you mean." When I first traveled to the Water Cave I thought it peaceful, tranquil even. However, once Mark shared with me that Satan used the lake as a prison for those who disobeyed, it had lost its appeal. "Evan, you have to be willing to kill those...those demons down there."

He cracked his knuckles, a deep sadness reflected in his eyes. "You've changed."

It wasn't the first time I heard those words over the last few days. "I've had no choice," I answered.

"Yeah, I guess not." His large brown eyes looked up at me with the sorrow of a child. "I'm sorry this happened to you."

"It happened to all of us." Trying to stay on track I added, "Let's meet in the training room in an hour, and we will work through the morning. Then we will have a sit-down with the Geeks. Also, you need to call your parents. They should be here. Tomorrow we transport. I wish we had more time, but we don't."

He looked at me with his overly confident grin and said, "Let's do this."

"Yeah, let's do this," I replied warily.

Chapter Twenty-One

No Choice

The clock read three a.m. as I lay in bed trying to make sense of life and what I was about to do. Each trip to Hell had been proven to be worse than the one before. I eventually realized that I survived my first visit only by the grace of the Lord. Of course, that was also most likely the case with each subsequent visit.

Panic built inside of me until I felt like a jack in the box ready to burst through its door. Anticipation of my skeleton flying from my flesh plagued my mind. Anxiety built up inside of me. The best thing to do was to ready myself for what was to come.

But how? I have nothing. The Mezirot would be well protected and the likelihood of survival was slim, which I would be reminded of at the meeting, better known as the "yell at Meadow-fest" a few short hours later.

Beth started. "Are you crazy?"

"You can't keep doing this!" Cassy chimed in.

"Meadow." Bubba shook his head in disappointment.

Mrs. Parker—the voice of reason—spoke, "She has no choice unless we want to sit back and watch the boy die." Mr. Parker said nothing but nodded his head in agreement with his wife.

"While I don't want Meadow and Evan to go, it must be done to save the boy," Dr. Wright said in his for-the-name-of-science voice.

"The boy." I didn't understand why it was so hard for any of them to call Mark by his name. Of course, they didn't know him as I did. They didn't know how sweet and good he was, how kind and gentle. What they saw was a monster ready to attack, a chore for them to monitor. Because Mark had grown incredibly wild, they had taken to tranquilizing him a majority of the day. The Geeks said it was to protect him, but I'm sure it was to give them peace.

Evan's mother chimed in. "My son will have nothing to do with this," looking down her crooked nose at me. Her lips curled into a snarl as if I were dog mess on the bottom of her shoe. "If she wants to behave recklessly then let her, but I don't see why our Evan is being dragged into this."

"Mom, stop," Evan pleaded. "I'm an adult now, and I made the choice to help Meadow. I won't walk away from this." His final words were a direct slam at his mother and father for walking away from the compound, from the Geeks.

Mr. Jacobs' face went deathly white, but Evan's mother wasn't done with her hate-filled words. "I will...I will call the police and have them shut this entire operation down."

"Wow!" Dr. Wright stepped in between Evan and his mother. "Are you crazy? Call the police? The Ganders would find and kill us all in a matter of days. They likely have followers on the force. No one would be safe, your son included. Don't forget that he is almost as valuable as Meadow."

Evan's mom looked away haughtily, but she knew Dr. Wright spoke the truth. If she did something so foolish as to involve any outsider into our mess, she may as well buy burial plots for her entire family.

"Son," she petitioned Evan again, "let her go. Forget about this girl," her voice filled with venom. "There are millions of girls out there. She's not worth this." Mrs. Jacobs' face crumpled—she snatched his hands into hers. "Don't do this, please. You're killing me."

My heart was crushed with each word she spoke, the soul-wrenching cries of a mother falling apart was horrible to witness. These were people I had grown up with—people who had once loved me as much as I loved them. The lump in my throat grew, and I stared at the wall straight ahead, trying not to allow their pain to become my own. There were hundreds of things I wanted to say—some good, some not so good, but I knew Mrs. Jacobs would rather not hear from me at all.

Evan shook his head, pulling his hands from his mother's grasp. "I'm not a coward, and I'm going to help Meadow. As a child you forced this life on me. It's all I know, and I will see it through." He looked over at me. "I happen to think she's worth it." Smiling sadly, I felt his eyes linger on me, but I continued to look away.

"You're all crazy." His mother slammed her hands against the closest table, then stormed from the room. Evan's father followed her out, his body sagging as he left.

I waited until they were gone. "Evan…"

"Don't let them get in your head, Meadow. This has to be done."

"I know, I was going to say you need to fix things with your parents before we go. I refuse to leave until you make peace with them."

He shook his head but stood to follow his parents. "Don't take what they said to heart…"

"It's okay. I would feel the same if I were them." My words caught in my throat. Evan stood back, waiting to see if I had more to say. "Go on," I shooed him with a flick of my hand. "Meet me in the transport room as soon as you can."

Evan patted me on the shoulder as he passed by. I smiled at him, then turned to the Geeks. "Let's prepare for transport. This time the setup will be slightly different since there are two of us."

Turning to my best friend, I said, "Cassy, try to understand." She glared at me for a long time, then looked away, her arms crossed over her chest. She would cool down at some point but there was no use wasting my time and effort until she did. Cassy was the most stubborn person I knew.

Looking back to the Geeks, I jerked my head towards the door. "Let's go." The entourage of doctors followed me. Shaking my head, I was still surprised they listened and followed my direction.

Warily I walked to the transport room, the walk feeling like my last. It was as if the Geeks were my warden and beyond the door of the transport room held my demise. I was scared for myself but terrified of Evan's fate. If he got hurt I couldn't live with myself. The thought sent my heart racing; my legs almost buckled underneath me.

Dr. Wright held the door open for me and grabbed my upper arm to steady me. I rested my hand on the door frame, knowing there was no time for weakness. Straightening my back, I pushed my fear deep down and marched into the transport room.

The Geeks grew quiet, assessing if I were up to the task. Turning to them, I addressed their fears. "I'm fine."

"Mead…" Beth started.

"No, really I'm fine. This is it, the last visit. Then I can heal, rest, find peace. Just one more time in that terrible place…then things will get better."

"How do you want to do this?" Dr. Ross asked.

"We need to be hooked up to monitors and I.V.s in case one of us doesn't return right away. Push the cots next to one another…make sure you have all the supplies needed to keep us going, just in case. Beth, I will need you to be super alert to our needs. If something happens to both Evan and me at the same time, you will need all hands-on-deck. Have some backup in case we need them—the Parkers if you can. The Romano family has been through enough and the Jacobs family may not stick around."

"Got it," Beth said.

"Dr. Wright, please continue watching over Mark and Dr. Ross…the Romano's could use someone just to…be there."

The Geeks jumped into action and did as I asked. It was crazy watching them follow my orders, surreal. Evan walked in as we finished setting the room to order.

"You okay?" I asked, looking him over.

"Oh yeah, I'm fine." Evan laughed nervously.

"And your parents?"

"We're all good."

I didn't believe him but there was no time to get into it now—maybe later.

Beth called to me from across the room. "Meadow, come back this way with me so I can stick the electrodes to your chest." I followed her into a tiny bathroom attached to the lab.

Dr. Ross took care of Evan. "Well, lay back, buddy. We will start with you while Beth takes care of Meadow." Evan nodded and laid back on his cot.

"How are you holding up?" Beth asked as she attached electrodes to my clavicle.

"I…uh…well I feel…"

"Torn, guilty, responsible?"

What the...I guess she isn't wrong. "Yes, I mean I loved Evan at one time, and he is sacrificing everything for me. But what if something happens to him? What if something happens to me and we don't fix Mark?"

"Listen, you have to put more trust in God and less in yourself. You're not in control, God is. You do trust in Him, don't you?"

"Of course, I do. It's just...I mean I do but...why is any of this necessary? Why do I have to repeatedly get my butt kicked by demons and watch the people I care about suffer? What good can come of any of this? Why would God make me go through this?"

Beth looked at me long and hard before she answered. "I don't know God's plan, but I bet when Joseph was in the bottom of the cistern where his brothers threw him, life looked a little bleak. And you know what happened to Joseph?"

"He became second to Pharaoh?"

"Yes, and that was a great accomplishment, but he helped the people of Egypt stay fed in a time of famine. Think of the lives he saved. I'm sure Joseph's plan was to remain at home and have a normal life but even before he was born, it was in God's plan for him to do great things. His road to greatness was tainted with pain, sorrow, and fear, but God delivered him through it. Imagine what He has planned for you. God trusts you; He loves you."

"Thank you, it's hard to see things in the midst of a storm, but you're right." I knew she was right. God had a plan and I needed to exercise my faith.

Beth smiled.

"All done. Let's get this show on the road."

We stepped out of the attached bathroom. As soon as I walked back into the transport room, I stopped in my tracks. Hovering over Evan's cot were his mother and father. I swallowed hard, too frightened to make a move. At one time I had loved those people and thought they would one day be my family.

Unfortunately, Evan's mother now had ill feelings towards me. Her beady brown eyes burned into mine. If she had reservations about me before, she loathed me now. My face grew hot and my stomach churned. *What could I expect? Her son is literally following me into the pits of Hell from which he may never return.*

"Meadow," Evan's father nodded curtly.

"Sir," I said, nodding back at him. I was glad to see he didn't appear to hate me—much.

"What you two are doing is crazy. You're children! There is no way you will win this fight," Mr. Jacobs said.

I bit my lip, considering if I should say anything back to him. I had to.

"With all due respect, I believe we can win this fight, and I think we can save an innocent soul here. Evan has a choice. He doesn't have to go. However, he has offered his help to me, and as much as I hate to admit it, I need him. You should be proud of your son's bravery. After all, you both had a hand in making us into what we are. Now we're finishing it. If you care for your son, maybe you can work with these guys here to find a way to undo what you have created."

They both flinched at my words. I wasn't trying to hurt them, but they needed to be reminded why we were in this situation.

"Can we have a few moments alone with our son?" Unwilling to admit defeat, Mrs. Jacobs spoke with words so cold I felt an icy current of hostility wash over me.

"Of course," I backed away and huddled with Dr. Ross and Beth. Dr. Wright stayed near the Jacobses.

"Do you think they will talk him out of it?" Beth asked.

"No, Evan is hard-headed and rebellious. He'll go if only to spite them."

"You're some brave kids," she said in awe, shaking her head. "Oh good, they're leaving," she added in a hushed whisper.

Evan's mother and father were being ushered out of the room by Dr. Wright. Mr. Jacobs had his arm wrapped around Evan's sobbing mother. My stomach knotted up, wishing my own parents had cared for me more than they had the Devil.

Evan's head sunk into the down pillow the Geeks provided. He was staring at the ceiling tiles, his hands resting lightly on his chest. "You okay? You don't have to do thi—"

"I know I don't have to, but I want to. Let's get started so we can get this over with." His voice cracked, and he turned his head away from me.

"Okay." I lay down on the cot next to his. Beth came over and deftly hooked wires to the electrodes she had attached to me moments before. Then she hooked me up to an I.V. while Dr. Ross prepared Evan for transport.

By the time she and Dr. Ross had us completely hooked up, Dr. Wright was back and double checking everything. "You two ready?" he asked.

We both nodded, unable to speak.

"Remember what I said, Evan. It's a large dark cavern. The lake goes on further than you can see. It has a—"

"Greenish glow? Yeah, I got it after you explained it the hundredth time and then there was the picture you drew…although a detailed PowerPoint presentation would have driven the point home nicely."

"Hush," I said, swatting his hand lightly with my fingertips.

"Okay, guys, time to relax." Dr. Ross stood above us. "We will inject you both with a mild sedative that will help you nod off, but it has a short half-life, so it won't hinder your ability to transport back. If you don't transport next to one another, meet in the Water Cave. Wait for as long as you reasonably can for the other. If your partner does not show, come back to your body and we will try again. Got it? If you get separated, Evan go back to the Water Cave and wait for Meadow. She will go back there first to find you before she transports back here. We refuse to lose either one of you." Dr. Ross looked at us pointedly. "Do you understand?"

Evan swallowed deeply and nodded as I closed my eyes and muttered a prayer for protection.

"Alright, guys. Beth and I will start the injections now. You will drift off rather quickly. Good luck."

Evan and I intertwined fingers and squeezed tightly. Beth stood next to me, watching my monitor but I didn't look at her. Instead, I turned to Evan. His head fell limply to the side and he looked at me. Before I drifted off, I thought I read his lips say, "I love you."

Chapter Twenty-Two

Keep Going

When my eyes opened, I was crouching down on the pebbly floor of the Water Cave. Brushing myself off, I glanced around the cavern. I appeared to be alone; there were no fiends around. There was no one. *NO ONE!* *Where is Evan?* I frantically searched the cave.

A rapid movement behind one of the slick beige stalagmite formations caught my attention. I bent around the shiny rock to examine what lay behind it. Suddenly a strong pair of arms grabbed me from behind and lifted me into the air.

A squeal escaped my lips just as a large hand clamped over my mouth. With all my might, I brought my elbow crashing down on the being. Bones cracked, forcing it to loosen its grip, dropping me onto the rocky ground.

"Meadow, it's me," Evan said in a harsh whisper. "Man, I think you broke a rib. You're stronger than I thought."

I smiled smugly. "Well then, I suggest you not creep up on me like that! Where were you?"

"There is a path that leads behind the lake over there." He pointed to a path I hadn't noticed before.

"I wonder where it leads," I asked intrigued.

"Now is a good time to find out," Evan replied.

"Wait...I don't want to lead us down a bad path, and we don't have time to just explore the caves of Hell."

"In essence, no path is good in Hell."

I shrugged. He wasn't wrong.

"If you want to save that *boy,* then we need to get in and get out."

I rolled my eyes at the emphasis he placed on the word boy.

"Yeah." I knew why I was here, but an overwhelming reminder of my last visit crippled me. Knowing that at some point, we would have to fight an undetermined number of fiends before we could go home almost doubled me over. *It is all for Mark…all for Mark.*

"You okay?" Evan asked.

"I—the last time I was here was—rough," I said. A flood of emotion filled my soul as I thought of my last visit.

Evan walked over to me and placed his hands on my shoulders, forcing me to look up. "You can do this, Meadow. A year ago, you were different. But now? Look at you. How many times have you made it down here and prevailed over the worst kinds of evil."

"I didn't have a choice."

"Of course you did, but you chose to kick butt and take control. This whole situation would have no structure if you weren't bossing all of us around."

"I'm not bossing anyone around." Crossing my arms over my chest, I tried not to smile. He was teasing me. Cassy, Bubba, and Evan had accused me of being bossy since cradle school. Some things never changed. The Geeks would probably agree with my friends' assessment of my demanding demeanor.

"Seriously, you have kept the rest of us strong in the face of tragedy. If not for you, we would all be scratching our heads waiting for the Geeks to come up with some half-brained plan which would likely not work. I heard about the piñata fiends in the simulation…" We both chuckled.

"Stop…"

"No, I mean it…" He continued with his flattery.

"No, hush. Do you hear…" A rustling came from the nearest opening.

"Hurry, let's go behind the lake."

"No, we're too exposed. Look, there's a crevice we can fit down in. Go, go. They're too close."

We dove for the crevice but there wasn't enough room for us both. Evan was too large. His eyes roamed the room, but time had run out. Four fiends walked into the room.

"Do what you need to do, I love you." He bent down and kissed my forehead, then he sprinted towards the lake, sacrificing himself for Mark and me.

"Come get me, you red goons," he yelled.

Biting my lip, I concealed a groan, his line cheesy yet effective. Fiends are incredibly fast–they caught up to Evan in no time.

"Well, what do we have here?" One of the monsters asked.

"Wouldn't you like to know, you red sack of...oomph." The second fiend punched Evan hard in the stomach, dropping him to his knees.

I peeked up from my hole, ready to pounce. Two fiends held Evan's arms behind his back while the others beat him. Just as I was about to jump out of hiding to pound some demon heads, someone else entered the room and sauntered over to my hiding place.

"Stop, you fools! Don't kill him. The boy may be of importance to us. It's obvious he is a transporter." My evil grandfather, Ray, stood above me. He looked down and winked. "Take him to my chambers. I need to search the area to ensure there are no more transporters lurking around." Ray dismissed the fiends.

"Whatever," one of the hateful monsters hissed, kicking Evan's legs out from under him. Evan once again fell to his knees, but he didn't give the fiends the satisfaction of crying out. Ray wandered around the room, pretending to search for more transporters. There was scuffling and something heavy dropped. Evan groaned, then all went silent. Biting on my knuckles, I waited until Ray and I were alone.

"Be careful with the boy. If you kill him, I will drag you straight to the Cave of Darkness."

Ray chuckled as the fiends wailed at his threat. Peeking from my hiding spot I could see they had an unconscious Evan by his arms and legs. They were carrying him away from the Water Cave.

"Well, you have been here all of what? Three minutes, and your help has already been caught. Good job," Ray drawled, clapping his hands lightly.

"Thanks for your underwhelming amount of support." I climbed out from my hiding spot.

"What's the plan?" he asked, his head tilted to the side and his brows raised in an I-told-you-so attitude.

"I need help," I implored.

"I can't do much for you. You have to decide whether you save your friend or take back the Mezirot."

"The Mezirot must come first, no matter what."

"I know that the Dark One has the Mezirot where the Water Cave and Fire Cave meet."

"How do you still have favor with Satan? By now he has to know you have helped me."

"Because I told him I have been helping you…I just leave little tidbits out here and there." Ray shrugged, deceit being the norm in his world. "He believes I misled you while creating a relationship with you. He hopes you will trust me, so I can manipulate you to his will."

"Are you?"

"Pardon?"

"Are you misleading me?"

"If I were, I wouldn't likely divulge that information to you now, would I?" Ray answered testily.

Not in the mood for an argument, I let it go. Raking my hand across my face I asked, "Which way do I go?"

"See that path there?" Ray pointed to the path Evan had shown me moments before. My stomach tightened. If I had listened to him we would still be together.

"Yeah," I sighed loudly. Wherever Ray was sending me was going to be awful.

"Go down that path and take the second tunnel on the left. It's a good half-mile walk. Follow the tunnel until you see a small but deep triangular hole in the ground. Squeeze through the shaft and allow yourself to fall to the bottom. It's quite a drop but you will be okay. From there you will be on the back end of the Fire Cave. You will come to a doorway guarded by two fiends. Kill them both, but you must do so without alerting anyone on the other side of the door."

"Ray…I don't want to kill them," I protested, even though I knew demon killing was part of the deal.

"Sounds like a personal problem," was his terse reply.

"Is there no other way?" I asked.

He hesitated for a fraction of a second. "Here," he pulled a glass orb from his pocket.

"What is it?" I looked at the orb. A gray smoky substance swirled inside itself.

"Something dear to me. You will be taking a risk using it. Once you defeat the fiends guarding the entrance to the chamber where the Mezirot is being held, enter the stone doorway. Fiends gather there so you must be quick. Cause a scene. Let the fiends surround you, as close as they can get, then throw the orb to the ground, smashing the glass. The gases inside will temporarily freeze all living beings in the room. You want to hold your breath until you exit the room, or you risk becoming frozen and getting caught. Grab the Mezirot and slide behind the tapestry of Satan surrounded by his fiends. There is a hidden opening there; go through that tunnel."

"Where does it lead to?"

"The Cave of Darkness," he said with a sigh.

"Oh, Lord." My body sagged. I couldn't go back there. The thought of being encompassed by the cursed darkness, even with the Mezirot, overwhelmed me.

"That's not the worst of it. You will be in the farthest, deepest part of the cave, a good three miles from the main entrance. If you succeed, you must transport back immediately, or Satan will torture you if he catches you."

"Why can't I come back this way?"

"There are fiends patrolling the area quite heavily, plus your mother would love to get her hands on you. The danger that lies in the Cave of Darkness will be less than the dangers that are here for you now, especially once word about your transporter friend circulates."

"I'm going to die," I said numbly.

"Yeah…that is likely." Ray looked far off into the distance. "That is all I can do for you. There is no other way unless you go back now and save yourself."

"No." I shook my head vehemently.

Ray nodded, knowing I would refuse. "Well, this is where I leave you. I can give you an hour to get to the Fire Cave. I will hide the boy as long as I can; however, soon my master must know he's here. The fiends won't keep quiet long. It would be of much greater benefit for me to be the one to expose his whereabouts. Good luck, child."

"An hour to get through this tunnel system, kill some fiends, and make it three miles through the Cave of Darkness?" I squealed. *Is this guy for real?*

Ray nodded. "When you get to the Cave of Darkness, send me a signal and I will help with a shortcut if I can." My panic was lost on Ray; however, I believed he really was helping as much as he could.

"Thank you." I walked over to the old man, hugged him, and planted a kiss on his rough red cheek. This could be my last time seeing my grandfather.

Ray pulled back in surprise. His hard eyes softened, and his ever-tense body relaxed for a fraction of a second. "Go." he pointed his gnarled finger at the path leading me to the backside of the Fire Cave.

My legs moved faster than they had in a while. I had been cooped up in the Geeks' lair for far too long and running felt nice. For the first time ever, I was glad my soul could feel the same sensations my body could while in Hell.

It didn't take long for my legs to ache, but I pushed on. I had to make it to the Mezirot. Ray's plan was dangerous and seriously flawed. In his plan, there was no room for me to rescue Evan.

Chapter Twenty-Three
A Fight at the End of the Tunnel

The windy tunnels Ray recommended I crawl through would have been fantastic had I been a toddler. Some of the turns were so sharp, I had to wiggle on my side like a worm. Not normally a claustrophobic person, the rocky walls closed in on me forcing panic to flow through my soul. At times the walls were less than an inch from my face. I would have turned back but I could not wriggle back out of the tight spots. It was easier to press on.

Before I reached the hole Ray had described, the tunnel opened back up. I was able to stand and walk normally, although my muscles and shoulders were stiff from dragging my body through the tiny area for so long.

The triangle hole was barely big enough for me to crawl through, but lucky for me a ladder made of rock descended to the bottom. If I had to drop the entire way down as suggested by Ray, I may have gotten hurt.

The air became humid as I traveled down the ladder, and the scent of sulfur filled my nose. Within seconds my entire body dripped with sweat. I tried to wipe my hands one at a time on my training suit, but the material wasn't absorbent.

Once I reached the bottom of the shaft, I peeked around to see if I could find the doorway Ray had described. The door wasn't visible, but ten feet ahead was a turn in the tunnel and a light shone dimly from around the corner. I peeked around the edge and spotted the door; however, the entrance wasn't protected by two fiends as Ray had described.

Instead, four red monsters guarded the door. Judging by my two-second glance they were fiends on steroids. Most fiends stood around 5-foot-5-ish and were lean, but these guys had to be closer to six-feet-tall, and muscle upon muscle popped from their arms and chests. Perched upon three of the monsters' heads were helmets made of skulls.

My heart pounded—I needed a plan. There was *no way* I could take on four massive fiends by myself. They would tear me apart, quite literally. Suddenly, I remembered the orb Ray had given me. Dared I drain the orb's power prematurely? If I used the orb now, I risked being overcome once in the Fire Cave.

Part of me wanted to flee but images of Mark and Evan being lost to me filled my mind. Satan had surely become aware of Evan's existence by now and was likely torturing him to find out my agenda. Even if Evan hadn't cracked, I knew the devil had a way of finding one's darkest secrets and fears. Since he had dug into my mind and used my deepest pain against me before, I wondered what he would use against Evan. *Would I be a part of his weakness?*

Scanning the area, I spotted a sinkhole. If I could hang from the ledge unnoticed, maybe I could get most of the fiends to move away from the door by throwing a rock, causing a distraction.

Tearing a piece of fabric from the arm of my training suit, I snagged it to a rock on the stairs at the bottom of the shaft, leading back to the Water Cave. Maybe the fiends would believe I had retreated. It was worth a try, and it was all I had.

"Ray, I'm here and am about to do something kind of stupid. If all works well, I will have the Mezirot in my hand in less than five minutes."

I waited for a reply but—nothing. Oh well, I would figure out the rest later. Scooping up a few pebbles and putting them in my pocket, I climbed down the sinkhole holding on tight. Once I had stabilized myself, I held on with one hand and fished the rocks from my pocket—a feat I had thought would be much easier than it was. Chucking the rock as hard as one could who was hanging onto a ledge for dear life, I caught their attention.

"She is here," one of the fiends cried out in excitement.

"Go look," another monster demanded.

"No, you go look," argued the first.

"All three of you go before I rip your hearts out and have them for dinner. Idiots, if it's the girl, she has a head start now." As they argued, my muscles throbbed and ached. My shoulders quivered.

Three fiends ran around the corner and down the corridor, not noticing the scrap of material I left as a clue for them. *Shoot.* Using my shaking muscles to haul myself up, I heard the patter of tiptoes coming from the direction of the Fire Cave door. Quickly I dropped back down out of view. "You're still here, aren't you?" the fiend asked.

Pressing my lips tightly together, I didn't make a sound. *Had the monster seen me?* My fingers—wet with sweat—began to slip from the ledge. A sharp pain seared through my arms, and sweat poured into my eyes. If I fell, I would be stuck for good.

The fiend walked around looking for clues to my whereabouts. He stopped, scrunched up his face and sniffed the air. He tilted his head, and finally noticed the fabric I left stuck onto the ladder. He grabbed it and climbed up the stone rungs. Silently swinging my legs up and over the ledge, I rested on all fours waiting for my arms to regain feeling.

Just as I felt strong enough to stand, a slap to the side of my head jarred my insides. The impact forced me forward two feet, my face breaking my fall. The fiend didn't give me time to recover before he went at me.

"I told you not to try and take the Mezirot back from me, you filthy girl." Each word was punctuated with a punch to the face. It was the fiend who had helped me through the Cave of Darkness. Grateful he was older and smaller than the others, I believed I stood a chance.

I rolled backwards, giving myself space to hop back to my feet. This guy was going to get it. I came at him with fists flying, kicking and clawing at the monster. But none of my efforts slowed him down.

The fiend and I fought for our lives, our tactics sloppy. For every three punches swung, we may have landed one. Clearing my mind, I crouched down to miss a wild punch the monster threw. Then springing into the air, I almost executed a perfect flying jump kick, but the fiend grabbed my leg mid-air and wrenched it so hard to the side I thought he had dislocated my femur from my hip. Falling on my side, I hit the ground and my vision distorted, giving the fiend the upper hand.

"You will rot down here, kid. I will hide you where even your grandfather won't find you." I raised my head, trying to see the monster as it stalked me. Lifting my left arm to protect my face, I thought about giving up, then an idea came to me—Superman.

A game Cass and I had played as kids. One of us would lay on our backs with legs extended in the air while the other laid their belly on their feet, pretending to fly. When we grew overenthusiastic, one of us would send the other sprawling butt-over-head three feet across the room. It was a wonder we had never broken a bone.

"Come on, finish me then," I said through clenched teeth, using my arms to pull my torso across the rocky ground.

The monster dropped to all fours and slithered on top of me. I dropped flat on my back. Rows of yellow jagged teeth were ready to tear my flesh apart. He grabbed my hair and jerked my head back, exposing my neck to him. Leaning back, I curled my legs into my body wedging my knees between us and kicked with all my might.

Just as I had hoped, the fiend went flying over the ledge. Unfortunately, I had twisted my mane into a tight knot on the top of my head before transporting and he grabbed it as he went over. My body slid across the earthen ground and came to a stop at the ledge where the demon hung by a wad of my hair. My neck hit the ledge sending pain down my back.

"Get off me! Get off!" I screamed. I wildly batted my fist behind my head in hopes of knocking the fiend off me.

My bun began unraveling, but the beast still dangled from my hair. Turning my body the best I could, I reached into my hair, prying the fiend's fingers from my locks. Thank goodness my hair was long, long enough that I could roll around and pull the nasty demon's hand to my mouth. Sinking my teeth into its scaly red flesh, a bitter acidic taste filled my mouth.

The fiend screamed, let go, and plunged deep into the dark hole. The bottom must have been pretty far down–I could barely hear the beast's final obscenities before it struck the ground. Then the room went silent.

Haggard, I curled into a fetal position, lazily wiping the fiend's blood from my mouth. My stomach curled at the sight of the tar-colored fluid that coated the back of my wrist. The thought of that being inside my mouth caused me to gag.

Tiny pebbles were cutting into my face as I lay motionless on the ground. In the distance, the other fiends could be heard approaching from the corridor. They must have abandoned their search.

Knowing my body couldn't withstand another fight, my only hope of passage was to outsmart the fiends. To overpower the beasts, I needed them to follow me into the Fire Cave, then I could use the glass sphere Ray had gifted me. It was a wonder the orb hadn't broken during my struggle with the fiend.

Walking around the corner near the stone door, I ran my hands along the devilish hieroglyphics depicting pharaoh fiends and beasts from long ago. Gently I pushed the rock door open a teensy crack to see what lay in wait for me. At least fifteen fiends roamed around the room—some wrestling with one another while others sat around stone tables and chatted. It was like an ancient demon hipster hangout.

Fiends were notorious for being quick; I needed to be quicker. Peering around the corner I could see the fiends approaching the stone ladder.

"Where do you think she went?" one of the large red monsters asked.

"She probably got scared and ran for—"

"Hey guys, looking for me?" I asked, sauntering around the corner with my hands on my hips. Yeah, and I thought Evan was lame with his lines, but it worked.

The fiends took no time in chasing me down. I flew through the door with dumb, dumber, and dumbest on my heels.

Head first I tripped into the room full of fiends. Each one of the creatures stood stock still, their mouths hanging open at the sight of me and their buddies bursting through the door. I scanned the room and quickly found what I was looking for.

A jagged stone pillar about four feet high stood in the middle of the room. Perched on top of the pillar in all its ragged glory was the Mezirot. I couldn't believe my luck. *How could they leave it laying out in the open like that? How could Satan trust these goons with the Mezirot?*

An extremely old fiend with grayish skin and pale gray eyes stepped between my view of the precious piece of fabric. He was unlike the other fiends in many ways. For one thing, he wore clothing, a long silver robe with golden swirls throughout. I wondered if he held a position of power over the others.

"What do you think you're doing, girl?" The fiend's mouth curved into a vicious smile.

"I'm taking that with me." I pointed to the Mezirot.

The fiend chuckled. "Do you think you will overpower us all?"

"I do," I answered, looking directly into the gray pupil-less eyes.

"Well, try your best then." The fiend lifted both arms over his head, daring me to make my move. The roomful of fiends gathered in a tight circle around me. Instead of sinking down into a fighting stance I allowed my left hand to go limp and drop inside my pocket.

"You will fall to my feet and beg for mercy," I spat at the old creature.

The fiend turned his back to share a laugh with his friends. Pulling the orb from my pocket, I balanced the tiny glass ball on the palm of my hand. The fiends grew serious as a devilish smile spread across my face. One by one their laughter faded until the older fiend turned and lunged at me. His red wrinkled face cried out, "Where did you get that!"

Without hesitation, I threw the glass ball down with all my might. With a faint tinkle the fragile ball burst, releasing the gray fog. The mist filled the room momentarily obscuring my vision. Pulling in a deep breath, I watched as each fiend grew still.

One by one they froze, some running towards me and some away. A burning sensation radiated throughout my chest. I needed air.

Careful not to step on any of the fiends, I wound my way through the maze to the Mezirot. The old robed fiend kneeled at the pillar in his final attempt to protect it. He turned to me and said, "You're no better than the rest of us, using dark powers to kill…"

Then he too fell over. My heart skipped a beat, but Ray had said they would only be frozen temporarily. The old fiend's enormous bulbous eyes remained open, staring into nothingness.

Tufts of white hair stuck out around his elfin ears. *Was the fiend mistaken?* As if reading my mind, the other fiends erupted into clouds of vapor and disappeared before my eyes. I stood in a room littered with fiend dust, bile crept up my throat. *Genocide. Was the old fiend right? Was I like them? Had I not just killed a roomful of beings?*

My lungs—nearly ready to burst—craved air. I snatched the Mezirot and exited behind the tapestry Ray had described to me. One day I would have to atone for what I had done but now wasn't the time. Once inside the Cave of Darkness, I allowed myself the opportunity to take in a deep breath of the amazingly stale air before I started the next leg of my journey.

Chapter Twenty-Four

A Race Against the Light

With the Mezirot clenched tightly in my hand, I used its light to navigate through the tunnels. My main obstacle would be making it to the entrance of the cave before the Mezirot's light died. If I had to wait for the powers to rejuvenate, then Satan would surely find and kill me.

As if reading my mind, Beth broke through my thoughts. "Meadow, are you okay?"

"I'm in the Cave of Darkness. Evan and I have been separated."

"Ray told me about Evan. You have to come back without him. Ray is keeping him safe for now, but you have to come back," Beth pleaded.

"I can't leave him here," I sobbed, despite knowing there was no other way.

"Let me put it this way," Beth plowed on hotly. "You have to make a hard choice. Mark is dying; his madness is literally killing him. You either get back here with the Mezirot and save him or you stay there risking yours and Evan's life on a suicide mission. If you think Satan will leave Evan unsupervised, you're crazy. Come back, heal Mark, then bargain with Satan through Ray. Maybe you can find a way to send the Mezirot back in exchange for Evan."

"I...I don't think..." I didn't know what to think. I was being asked to make an impossible decision.

"You don't have time to think. Make a choice and go. If you run out of light in that cave, all of you die."

I made the decision Evan would want me to make. "I'm coming back."

"Get going," she said, and then she was gone.

Determined to save Mark, I ran through the tunnels praying I would make it back to the Geeks' lair in time.

Chapter Twenty-Five

Evan

"Oh, God," Evan groaned, waking up. His arms were bound tightly above his head, and a burning sensation flowed through his shoulder blades. Pinpricks of pain ran from his knees to his legs; they too were wrapped in the thick, prickly rope.

"Hello, Evan," Nancy said.

"Wha...Mrs. Fields? What're you doing here?"

"Keeping you alive for now."

"Are...are you a transporter too?"

"No, I live here now," she answered simply, tugging at the ropes that bound his arms and legs, ensuring he couldn't escape.

"You...you're dead?"

"Meadow didn't share that with you? Hmm...I thought she would have at least felt a little sad over my passing."

"Must have slipped her mind," Evan mumbled.

"Yes, must have," Nancy snarled sarcastically. "Well, if I know my daughter, she won't let you stay here for long. She will come for you."

"No, she won't. I made her promise." Evan choked on the words, his throat dry.

"Apparently you underestimate how much she loves you."

"Not me," Evan whispered.

"Believe me. What she thinks she has with Mark isn't real. She loves you. She broke when you two split up. Did you know she locked herself in her room for months, crying and listening to one sad love song after another?" Shaking her head, she plowed on. "Binge watching heart-wrenching love stories while shoveling in as much ice cream as her little body could handle."

Evan didn't want to hear what Nancy said. It hurt, knowing the pain he had caused Meadow.

"She would give her life for yours even if she doesn't yet realize it. Did you know—"

"Stop," Evan shouted, cutting Nancy off.

"Poor girl, she had given up." Nancy wouldn't be stopped. "Until she started transporting, we thought they were just dreams. But then Mark showed up, and there was a change in her. I knew something was going on so I followed them. He would take her deep in the woods, encouraging her to practice transporting. Of course, she was too interested in the boy to do any good at honing her skills, but he gave her a reason to start living again."

Evan's heart ached at the thought of Meadow alone in the woods with *that boy*, the one she would fight Hell for. "Mrs. Fields..." Evan forced the words out of his mouth, the ceiling starting to spin. He was going to lose consciousness. "I'm dying..." He passed out before he heard her reply.

"Not yet, dear...not yet..."

*   *   *

"Dang it, Ray," I said aloud after I had tripped and fallen for the third time. "Why can't you help me?"

"Oh, but I can," he said, not in my mind this time but behind me.

"Ray!" I spun around.

My face lit up and I took two quick steps towards him but stopped short. I didn't know how to behave around him.

Ray looked terrible, his clothes tattered–bruises surrounded both eyes and lined his cheekbone. "What...what happened?"

"The Dark One knows I gave you the sphere of death. Apparently, he went to check on the Mezirot."

"I'm not too happy with you about that myself. I wish you had told me what that orb really did, Ray. I would have—"

"You would have what? What could you have done differently? There was no other way for you to defeat that many fiends in one go," Ray interjected defensively.

"Maybe so but I would have rather known up front."

"You have bigger issues than that right now. Getting out of here is priority. I still have your friend hidden, but that won't last long. I was sent here to find your whereabouts and report back to Satan."

"Why are you telling me this?"

"I'm trying to get you to safety if you will be quiet long enough for me to explain!"

"Be my guest." I curtseyed and waved my hand for him to continue.

"Terrible child…" Ray muttered under his breath. "I will get you to the entrance of the cave, but then I must go back to my master and turn your friend over to him. I have to gain back his trust. If I turn the boy in, he will see I gave you the sphere to make you think I was helping you. What are a few demons' lives if I can get Marcus back for him?" Ray didn't look upset, only resigned to his fate of slavery to the King of Darkness.

"Hmm," I huffed, crossing my arms.

"Let's go. The power of the Mezirot will fade soon."

"Fine." Remembering how miserable my last visit was I followed Ray through the winding tunnels of the cave, relieved I didn't have to find my own way.

"You know your way around well," I said. It struck me strange Ray would know how to navigate these tunnels. From the way I understood it, no one ventured into the Cave of Darkness by choice.

"I'm sure it will come as no surprise to you that I get myself into trouble from time to time. I use this place to get away. No one would ever come down here to find me."

"Can't Satan find you?"

"Sure, he could, but he won't waste his energy to hunt me down. He knows I will be back when I feel his anger has subsided. None of us are of much importance to him. If he were honest with himself, he would admit that even Marcus isn't that important, but it's more the principle that you stole him…"

"I never meant to…but it doesn't matter; I would do it again in a heartbeat."

"Foolish girl, you have no idea what could happen to you here."

I shuddered. "I wouldn't last long down here that's for sure."

"You would be surprised what you can do when you have no choice. I do worry about you, however," Ray shot over his shoulder as he turned a sharp corner, his condescending tone returning.

"What do you mean?" My short legs worked double time to catch up.

"You're in quite a pickle if you ask me. Once you get out of this cave, then you have to go home to save one boy while you leave one behind to rot for all eternity."

"Evan." His name fell from my lips and my chest hurt as if someone had smashed it with a hammer.

"Can you forget about him?" Ray asked nastily.

"Of course not," I spat. "I thought you would be able to protect him for me until I could formulate a plan to rescue him."

"Well, apparently that isn't the case as he will soon meet the Dark One."

"What do I do? If I go back to save Evan, I take the chance of killing him, Mark, and myself."

"Oh, I would leave him here, and save yourself." Ray dismissed my despair.

Ray's reasoning was selfish. *But are't I selfish as well? Did I not bring Evan here to save the boy my heart longed for? Who have I become?*

"I..."

"Don't think on it too hard, girl. Do the smart thing here. Save yourself, save Marcus. Go home and talk to Marcus. Give him an opportunity to weigh in on this. He is, after all, who the Dark One truly desires."

"It's not fair. Mark doesn't belong here."

"Doesn't he?"

"What's that supposed to mean?" I stopped in my tracks.

"All I'm going to say is you should ask the boy why he deserves this life."

I opened my mouth to argue, but then realized we had walked into a room with a great many tunnels spewing in several directions. *The entrance to the Cave of Darkness...how have we gotten here so quickly?*

The Mezirot still shone brightly, the bluish hue both beautiful and frightening at the same time. Ray noticed and instructed, "Put it in your pocket for a moment. There are a few things you should know."

Pushing the rough piece of fabric in my pocket, the room went black. "When you are weakened, clutch the Mezirot in your hand to regain momentary strength," Ray told me. "When in a dark place you will have temporary light, and to cure your friend's addled mind turn all the lights off in the room, clutch the Mezirot in your hand, and let the light do the rest. For now, that is all I can share. You will learn more if the need arises. Be smart. Go home and talk to Marcus, then decide what you should do for your friend, Evan."

Ray was right. I had to save Mark before it was too late. Beth said he didn't have much time left.

Once Ray was done talking, I pulled the Mezirot from my pocket and threw my arms around his neck. "Thank you, Ray."

Ray patted me awkwardly on the top of my head before he stepped away. I could have sworn his eyes were damp with tears, but it was hard to tell as they were no more than solid black spheres.

"Get out of here, kid," he said gruffly. "Be careful." I almost missed those final words because he said them so quietly.

"Yeah…thanks." Turning I walked through the threshold bracing myself for the onslaught of fiends that surely waited for me.

Chapter Twenty-Six

An Unfortunate Attack

Ready for an ambush I marched out of the Cave of Darkness prepared to fight. Spinning in a circle, looking for a mass of bloodthirsty monsters, I discovered nothing. Not one single fiend anywhere. *Strange*...I wondered if they would be waiting at the top of the gorge for me.

Stuffing the Mezirot back in my pocket, I took a few more steps away from the cave when something squeezed me around my midsection from behind. My entire body jerked backward, and I flew back into the Cave of Darkness.

Pounding my fists against the appendage around my midsection, I waged war against the being. Whatever held me captive was much stronger than I was. Mentally kicking myself for being hasty on putting the Mezirot away, I knew I would have to fight blindly.

Taking a moment to evaluate the situation, I ran my hand along the extremity that held me, thinking it would be the arm of a fiend. However, it wasn't. The more my hand roamed, the less I liked what held me. The thing encircling my waist was snakelike, but slimy and smooth. I estimated it to be at least twelve inches in diameter, and it was wrapped around my waist three times over.

The beast squeezed tighter. One of my ribs popped, and I choked out a cry for help. The only thing I could do was wriggle my fingers between the arm of the being and slide the Mezirot out of my pocket. It felt good to wrap my fingers around the cool scrap of fabric.

With as much force as I could muster, I pulled my arm out of the monster's grip and thrust the Mezirot into the air. "Ahhhh," I screamed, channeling my power through the cloth. Light brighter than ever before burst from the sacred piece of cloth.

A skull-shattering wail filled the cave, covering my battle cries. The shriek rattled the stone walls raining rock and dust upon us. The creature dropped me and slithered back a few feet. I landed on my back, my sight fading between light and dark. Quick to sit up, I captured my first glimpse of the monster.

The creature's head almost scraped the ceiling of the cave. Six snake-like tentacles protruded from all angles of its gelatinous frame. The monster used its extremities to pull its massive gray form in my direction.

Sprinting back to the mouth of the cave, I tried to make my escape. The creature was much quicker than its slovenly body would have led me to believe, and it wrapped its tentacles around my legs, flinging them out from underneath me. My chin smacked the stone floor with a sickening crack.

The thought of how my body held up on earth crossed my mind. In the past, my bodily injuries on earth weren't as severe as what my soul suffered in Hell, but they still hurt when I awoke. Despite the struggle—I kept a death grip on the Mezirot. If I lost it now, the beast would claim me.

Pumping my legs up and down I tried to wriggle free, but I was no match for this creature. Pulling me back into the cave, the monster lifted me into the air legs first. My head dangled above the ground, an enormous throbbing pressure pounding inside. The monster continued to lift me towards its mouth. Hundreds of layers of teeth lined its mouth all the way to its throat.

The creature lowered me into its wide-open jaws. I closed my eyes and waited for the painful gruesome death to overtake me. Anticipation of my body being torn to shreds paralyzed me.

"Use the Mezirot, you stupid girl," Ray's voice rang out.

Opening my eyes, I saw Ray anxiously hopping from one foot to the other. The monster continued to lower me into its jaws. Gooey gray slits opened to solid white pupils that glared hungrily at me. Not sure what Ray meant, I raised the Mezirot into the air again and slammed it into one of the creature's gooey eyes. Once again, I was dropped to the rocky ground. "Oomph," the air in my lungs fled my body.

The monster dove at me, but I rolled to the side. With little strength left, I willed all my power into the Mezirot. Extending both of my arms directly at the creature, I screamed. This time my war cry could be heard over its wail.

A beam of brilliant blue light shot from the fragment of fabric and hit the monster right in the middle of its jellified body which jiggled in waves of blue electric current. The being shook rapidly and the power of the Mezirot strobed.

My power waned, but I held steady. The monster's body swelled and the light strobed so fast, our shadows were cast over the wall like strange marionettes. Then, just as the light flashed for the last time, I stood with a renewed sense of strength, and the monster exploded. Bits of gray matter and putrid green goo covered the walls, Ray, and myself. The Mezirot went back to its normal pale blue illumination.

Stunned, I stood completely still, trying to process what I had seen, trying my hardest to un-see it. The Mezirot spit a small amount of light at Ray and myself.

"Well, that was splendid," Ray's voice echoed in the darkness.

"Not how I would describe what happened," I answered shakily, swiping the monster's slimy flesh from my body. "What was that?"

"A fiend eater."

"Um...oh. What?"

"There are many of them that roam the tunnels down here. As a rule, they don't make themselves known other than when they smell a fiend."

"I wonder why it came for me then?"

"Master has been so preoccupied with this Marcus situation that he hasn't sent many fiends down here for the fiend eaters to hunt."

"Well, that's...um...too bad?"

"The power you hold is extraordinary," Ray mumbled.

"It's the Mezirot." I shrugged.

"I'm not saying the Mezirot isn't without its perks, but you...you hold powers I didn't know about."

"Do you mean I created that light thingy?"

"Possibly..." He looked at me as if he were seeing me for the first time.

"Well, thanks for coming back for me."

"Go," he said, pointing his old gnarled finger to the exit.

The tiniest sliver of light from the Mezirot guided me to the mouth of the cave once again. Just out of curiosity, I tried to transport from where I stood but I could feel the wards that protected the Cave of Darkness preventing me from returning home. I would have to climb to the landing and leave from there.

My biggest fear was finding fiends at the top of the gorge; even one would be too many. The battles of the day had mentally and physically exhausted me. My body was bruised, ribs broken, and my jaw hung loosely to one side. The slime covering my body smelled of sulfur and decaying flesh, causing me to gag.

The climb up the rocky stairs was as daunting and exhausting as it had been before, but I climbed with a purpose. Standing at the landing, I questioned why there were no fiends in wait for me. Looking around, I saw that the landing looked as it always had. The wall torches lit with fire and the stone bridge leading to the Fire Cave was intact. *Why does it feel wrong?*

Rather than remain in Hell like a sitting duck, I transported back to my body. The familiar tug at my soul sent me spiraling back to the Geeks' lair. Immediately, I sat up and gulped in a lungful of sulfur-free air.

"Meadow!" Beth and Dr. Ross shouted at the same time. Everyone was there—Cassy, Bubba, Dr. Wright, the Parkers, the Jacobses.

"I'm okay, I'm okay…I have the Mezirot." Opening my palm, I dropped the Mezirot into Dr. Wright's outstretched hands.

"Why hasn't Evan awakened?" His mother asked standing over her son's body. She had his hand clutched in her own. His body had begun to turn pink. The change had started.

"I couldn't…he—" I stopped.

"Where's my son?"

"We…can fix this…" I stammered.

What could I say? Her worst thoughts had come to pass. I opened my mouth to apologize, but before the words could leave my mouth she leapt across the room, straddling my bed.

The commotion that ensued was more than my body could handle. I didn't pass out, but my world went black and it was several minutes before I came to. Bubba cradled me tight against his chest while I huffed and puffed.

My body shook with each ragged breath. We were in the hallway, no longer in the transporting room. I looked down at my hand and saw blood trickling from where my I.V. had been moments before.

Cassy stomped out of the transport room. "Serves her right for attacking you," she said.

"What...who?"

"Mrs. Jacobs, of course. It's not your fault what happened."

"What did you do, Cassy?" I asked, shocked she would disrespect Evan's mother.

Cassy looked at Bubba and nodded, her head indicating something down the hall.

"We need to get you cleaned up then we can talk. Let's go to your room where there are no prying ears."

Bubba easily swung me into his arms and carried me to my living quarters. He deposited me on my bed and took watch at the front door as Cassy picked me out some pajamas and handed me a few towels.

"Go change. I have some bandages for your hand when you get done—although I think the bleeding has stopped." Cassy grabbed my hand and examined it. Mechanically, I did as Cassy asked, wondering what I had done to my hand. My knuckles throbbed as I changed clothes.

"Come here," Cassy beckoned, her hands filled with bandages, gauze, and medical tape. I walked to her and held out my hand. She only needed the Band-Aid as there was no more bleeding, just a knot and the beginnings of a fabulous bruise.

"You okay?" she asked. I think I nodded 'yes'.

Cassy eyed me. "Dr. Ross said to give you two of these and leave you alone. Soooo take these and go to sleep. I'm staying on your couch. If you need me, holler. Okay?"

Truly, I wanted to be left alone, but exhaustion set in and I agreed. Taking the pills from Cassy's outstretched hand, I tossed them in my mouth and swallowed them dry. Then I snuggled into bed, ignoring Cassy's watchful eye. It wasn't long after my head hit the pillow that I fell into a deep, peaceful, and dreamless sleep.

Chapter Twenty-Seven

Bruised Ego

I would like to say I felt fully rested when I awoke, but I didn't. It was as if I had been awake for days on end. Nothing felt real, my head was heavy, and the world around me was different. Or maybe I was different.

"Meadow?" Cassy asked, coming to my bedside.

"I'm up," I tried to gulp but my mouth and throat were dry. "What happened?"

Cassy walked over and handed me a glass of water.

"Thanks," I smiled gratefully.

"Well, you almost killed Evan's mom last night, so we gave you enough sedatives to kill a horse. But aside from that, you just had a normal day living 500 feet underground fighting the demons of Hell."

I chuckled for a moment but then I squealed, "I did *what* to Evan's mom?"

"I mean she started it, but you sure put her in her place if you ask me." Cassy shrugged giving me her 'that's what she gets' look.

"Cass, what happened? What did I do?" I sat up, frantically yanking the blankets from my body.

"When you came back without Evan, his mom flipped. She jumped on your bed, slapped you around a bit then you...um, I don't know what you would call it, but you did some crazy ninja attack kicking her across the room... You jumped on top of her and Bubba had to pull you off."

"Oh, Lord, what have I done?"

"Don't worry, she's okay. I mean her ego may be bruised, but she had it coming. She acts like all of this is your fault. Yet, she forgets she was like the rest of them sticking needles into her baby's arms—into *our* arms. They were among the ones who kept us from having normal lives, and normal families."

"Oh!" The air rushed from my lungs. Cass, Bubba, Evan...we had all been orphans before the transporter experiments. Sometimes I forgot they too had been raised by people who experimented on them. "I'm...I'm sorry," I said, hoping my friend didn't think I was as selfish as I felt.

"Ah, she had it coming," Cass said again, dismissing me with a wave of her hand, not understanding what I had really been apologizing for.

Mrs. Jacobs' face popped into my mind driving away all other thoughts. "Where is she? I must apologize."

"Um, let's leave that for another time, shall we? She needs time to cool off. What you need to do is get dressed and go to the holding chamber." Cassy threw a set of training gear my way. "The Geeks don't know how to use the Mezirot to save Mark. And not to alarm you, but he's in bad shape. I'm afraid he won't survive much longer."

Throwing my legs over the side of the bed, I grabbed the clothing and changed quickly. I must have been in a major daze last night as I looked down at the pj set Cassy had given me. There was a large black cat on the shirt and the bottoms had footies with big black cat heads on both feet. When I took them off to change, I saw the words MEOW across the backside. Once our lives turned back to normal, I was going to burn the sleepwear Cassy had gifted me with.

Chapter Twenty-Eight

Saving Mark

Dr. Wright and Beth were already in the holding chamber. The Mezirot was laying on a microscope between them. I walked over to where Mark was caged. He was pitiful. His face twisted in pain, and his pale skin had turned a nasty shade of gray.

"Meadow, do you know how to use the Mezirot to save him?" Beth asked. I turned to look at her. Something in her voice bothered me. Exhausted, her normally youthful face sagged, and her eyes drooped. Shifting my gaze to Dr. Wright, I could tell he was worn down as well.

"You two need rest," I told them. "You will make yourselves sick."

"Soon, but right now focus on Mark." Beth answered.

Mentally I decided that once we got Evan back, I would take charge for a few days so the Geeks could rest.

"Turn the lights off, please," I instructed, then turned back to Mark, wondering if we were too late. His eyes were sunken into his head, and his breath was labored. His normally pale skin was sweaty and translucent. It was apparent by the way his skin hung from his face he had rapidly lost a lot of weight.

With the flip of a switch, the room went dark, except for a slight glow from the control panel. Concentrating with the Mezirot in my hand, the room lit up more brilliantly than it had in the Cave of Darkness, the light was more white than blue.

We waited, and nothing happened. "Maybe it takes a few minutes," I said doubtfully.

"Meadow, I think you will have to go into the holding chamber," Cassy said. I had forgotten she was in the room.

"I don't—" I began.

Dr. Wright interrupted. "You know I think Cassy's right. You may need to get closer."

"Meadow, don't," Beth pleaded. "Just because he looks frail doesn't mean he can't hurt you. You're weakened as well."

"We have to try. This may be our last chance to save him."

Beth clamped her mouth shut hearing the finality in my voice. Dr. Wright nodded his head towards the chamber.

"Stand by the door. I will open it long enough for you to get in and do what you need to do. If he gets out of hand I will sedate him."

"Okay." I walked to the chamber door, my legs trembling beneath me.

Dr. Wright pushed a large red button on the control panel. The lock on the door clicked and swung inward. I walked in and the door clanged closed behind me.

Mark knew I was there. His eyes trained on me, his body draped across his bed. With the Mezirot clutched in my hand at shoulder level, I crouched down next to him and allowed the light of the Mezirot to do its job. Within seconds Mark's skin lost its sickly luster and returned to his normal paleness. His body swelled with a renewed strength.

It was the renewed strength that was the main problem. In my naivety, I didn't realize that even though physically Mark was returning to normal, his mental state had stayed the same.

Before I could pull away, Mark snatched the Mezirot from my hand, holding it over his head. Jumping to my feet I tried to snatch the parchment from his hands, but he was much taller than me, and I couldn't reach it.

Pounding his chest with my fists in a last-ditch effort to regain possession of the only item that could cure his mental state, I started to panic. Mark smiled at me, his face full of malevolent joy at my despair. Helplessly I watched as he tore the Mezirot in half, then in quarters. The beige pieces of fabric rained down upon me, and I dropped to my knees.

Mark turned his focus on me. In the background, I heard Beth pounding against the glass—the sound like a drum inside my brain—warning me to run but I couldn't. Instead, I grabbed shards of the Mezirot and let them fall loosely from my fingers. *I have failed.*

Dr. Wright opened the door with a tranquilizer gun aimed at Mark. His first shot missed, and he frantically tried to reload another dart. Mark inched closer. The second dart hit its target. Mark fell, his body landing mere feet from me.

All I could do was gaze upon his sweet face before he drifted off into a drug-induced stupor. His eyes narrowed on me just as he drifted off; he whispered, "Meadow?" His eyes closed, and a sweet familiar smile spread across his face.

The Mezirot had worked.

Chapter Twenty-Nine

Anticipating a Visit

Waves of unrelenting heat washed over his soul, sweat coating every square inch of his body. His eyes stuck together, and he didn't have the energy to force them open.

"How long can he last down here?" A voice asked.

"I don't know, maybe a few days," a man's voice replied.

"Will she come back?" Evan recognized the voice as Nancy Fields.

The man spoke again. "I'm sure she will, but she isn't important in all of this. It's the boy we need."

"She's important to me."

"Oh, hang the loving mother act. You want her for what she can do for you down here." The man sounded more amused than angry, although his words were hateful.

"You're one to talk. Who helped her this entire time?"

"She would have never made it without my help. You didn't train her," the man said.

Evan kept his eyes closed, hoping to hear something useful.

"I was going to, but I didn't expect things to happen the way they did. As soon as she graduated, I was going to reveal her special gifts to her. It doesn't matter now. What's done is done."

"Yes, what's done is done..." the man answered, a smirk on his face.

*   *   *

"Meadow, Mark is awake now. He's asking for you." Dr. Ross sat down next to me on the bench outside Mark's room.

"How is he?" I asked not attempting to move.

"He's grief-stricken, but much better. I assume he is back to his old self. Seems like a nice guy." Dr. Ross smiled at me.

"He is," I agreed. Still, I made no attempt to stand.

Dr. Ross picked up on my hesitation. "What is it, Meadow? What's wrong?"

"I sit here outside a room where Mark receives five-star treatment while Evan is fighting for his life in the pits of Hell. It's hard to be happy for Mark when I don't know what's going on with Evan."

"Evan made a choice, you know."

"Yes, but his decision was clouded by his feelings for me, not some moral sense of right or wrong. His love for me is the only reason he transported. He gave himself over to save me…to save Mark. And now I don't even have the Mezirot as a bargaining tool."

Dr. Ross didn't ask for it, but I shared with him all that happened during my last transport. I started with Evan sacrificing himself for me, squeezing through the tunnels, fighting and unknowingly killing fiends, sharing a touching moment with Ray, and having the giant octopus monster blow up in my face. I talked until I was talked out. Dr. Ross was a good listener.

"You have to be the toughest person I know," he said. Seeing my doubtful look, he continued, "No, seriously, you're strong Meadow. Do you think God would allow you passage into such a dark place if it weren't true? He knew you could overcome the terrors of Hell."

"Will it ever end? I can't do much more. I'm losing myself. I feel like…like I have lost God completely. When I pray, I feel abandoned." I lowered my head, ashamed of my confession.

"God never leaves us, you know. In times like this, we need to draw closer to Him is all. With all the craziness surrounding your life, I'm sure there wasn't a lot of prayer time between kicking fiend butt and dealing with old crotchety grandfathers, huh?"

I snickered at his description of Ray. Old and crotchety was an understatement. "Yeah, I suppose. But we still have to figure out a way to help Evan."

"Are you up for another transport?" Dr. Ross's eyes seared into mine, concern permeating from his very being.

Shaking my head, I shared with Dr. Ross what had truly been bothering me. "That's the thing, Dr. Ross. I can't. This morning I snuck into the transporting room ready to save Evan, but I can't transport anymore."

Chapter Thirty

A Trade

Evan's head pounded but he kept his eyes closed, hoping to gain some knowledge from his captors.

"It has been too long; she's not coming," Nancy hissed.

"She will come. Give her more time," the old man replied.

"I mean it. Contact her, Ray. This boy is going to die down here. I give him two days tops."

"Forget it," Evan spoke up, reminding Nancy and Ray that he was still in the room with them. "Meadow and I made a pact. We promised to not come after one another if we got stuck down here. She won't come back."

"You obviously don't know my daughter. She will come back."

"I hate to tell you this, but she's not the same sweet girl you once knew, Mrs. Fields. Maybe you don't know her as well as you think."

"What do you mean?" Nancy asked, more annoyed than concerned.

"I mean, she found out her entire life was a lie. Her mother tried to kill her, her father is on the run after *murdering* someone she cared deeply for, she has endured multiple trips to Hell, more death, destruction…" Evan's voice cracked, "than any person should ever have to witness. I could go on, but I think you can see how such trauma would change a girl like Meadow."

"Hmm, she was more…harsh when I saved her from the Cave of Darkness, but I thought it was an act…Ray, what do you think?"

"How am I supposed to know? I never knew the girl. You made sure of that. I think she's whiny and weak," Ray spat.

"Then you don't know her either," Evan said, tugging at the ropes binding his wrist.

"True, but she is still a pain and not worth all of the trouble she has put me through."

"Who are you?" Evan asked, turning his head to look at Ray.

"Ray Gander, your girlfriend's grandfather." Ray stepped closer, so Evan could have a better look at him.

"Oh," Evan said, unimpressed, and turned his head to look up at the rocky ceiling. He had heard gruesome stories of Ray Gander throughout his life. From the time he was ten years old, his parents revealed to him the experiments at Ganders. It was then they shared with him that Meadow would need his protection—*from what exactly* had remained unclear for many years. Every day he trained to defend his friend alongside Bubba and Cassy. It was a heavy burden for children so young.

"She sure is lucky to have you all as family." Evan shifted his wrists trying to loosen the ropes again.

"Give it up, kid. You will never break free from those—unless of course, Meadow makes the trade." Ray chuckled.

"What trade?" Evan asked.

"Why you for Marcus of course," Ray replied, cutting his laughter short.

Evan stopped fighting, allowing his body to go limp. After all he had done to Meadow, she would never make a trade like that.

*   *   *

"What do you mean you can't transport?" Dr. Ross asked.

"It isn't happening." My shrill voice echoed through the hall. "I mean I don't know what to do. I have mastered transporting on demand, and it's like there is nothing there. Something is missing inside of me...like the transporter part is gone. I never knew it was there...but now it's missing."

"Can we...can I run some tests and see what is going on?" Dr. Ross's brow furrowed, and he chewed on the inside of his cheek.

"Sure, but can we keep this between us for now?"

"Of course," the doctor answered distractedly. "Let me gather some info. In the meantime, you go check on Mark." He checked his watch. "Meet me in lab one in say...thirty minutes."

"Okay," I nodded, fervently flicking my tears away with my fingers. Just behind me was Mark's room.

Taking a deep breath and viciously rubbing my hands over my face to erase traces of tears, I walked the few feet to his room. Before I was ready the glass doors slid open, granting me access. A rush of air hit my back as they closed behind me.

Mark was awake and watched as I walked in. Suddenly I was shy and didn't know what to say. "I see you got rid of your crazy."

He didn't crack a smile. I didn't blame him; it wasn't funny. Besides, he never got my jokes even when they were funny.

"How are you?" I asked. He shrugged his shoulders. "We were worried about you, you know?" Taking a few cautious steps closer I hovered over his bed.

Mark's room, for the time being, was in an uninhabited living quarter. It was similar to mine but set up more like a hospital room. The walls were blank and there was no other furniture except for his bed, a bedside table, and a wooden rocking chair.

He still didn't answer. My worry for him became increasingly intense, but I couldn't push. There was no telling what he had lived through these past few weeks. The darkness that compelled him must have been pure torture.

Plopping down in the rocking chair, I made no more attempts at conversation. The incessant ticking of the wall clock broke through the silence like a jackhammer. I wanted to run from the room; but running into Cassy or one of the Geeks would be worse than Mark's painful silence.

What would I say to them? How could I tell them Evan would likely die? Mark unknowingly destroyed the only bargaining tool I had had when he turned the Mezirot into confetti. Not that any of that mattered because I was no longer able to transport to make said trade anyway.

"Well, I have to go, and…meet with Dr. Ross. I will come back to check on you tonight." Mark barely nodded his head. He looked over at me, his eyes glazed with sadness. We had both changed through our experiences. I wondered if we would ever be able to find what we once had before all this madness.

A lump formed in my throat, preventing me from saying anything more. However, I didn't know if I *should* say anything. Mark had asked to see me, then acted as if I weren't there. Confused, I left the room, praying Dr. Ross would find the answer to my problems.

Chapter Thirty-One

Detached

"All done." Dr. Ross pulled the needle from the bend of my arm and pressed a cotton ball to the puncture site. "Listen, I want to run your blood immediately and figure this out. In the meantime, you need to rest. I asked Cassy to have dinner delivered to your room. Downtime is good, something you haven't had the courtesy of in a long while."

"When will we get the results?"

"Beth and I will come see you before bedtime. I should have some clue as to what is going on by then."

"Okay, I need to go see Mark I suppose..."

"Um, actually he asked...he asked for no visitors this evening."

Crushed, confused, and more than a little relieved, I bowed my head.

"Don't be upset, Meadow. He's been through a lot and needs time to sort things out."

"*He* needs time? I haven't had a moment of peace in weeks! I sacrificed my soul for his...for Evan..." and then it happened, the ugly cry face. Not the inconspicuous tears leaking from the corner of my eyes, but the putrid crumpled-up face of a heart in despair.

"Oh my," was all Dr. Ross said before putting his arms around my shoulders and comforting me for the hundredth time that day. The poor man would learn to avoid me like the plague if he knew what was good for him.

"Thanks." I pulled away. "Maybe you should start charging by the hour," I kidded.

"Maybe I will just be your personal therapist free of charge."

"I could handle that." I ran my arm across my eyes. "Thank you for being there. I don't know how I would be able to hold it together if it weren't for you."

Dr. Ross shrugged it off, but I saw his tan cheeks darken. He was a good man. I wondered why he and Beth didn't have children. They would make good parents.

*   *   *

Not intending to, I wandered back to Mark's room. I didn't go in but stood in the hallway watching him through the glass door. He lay the same way he had when I left him, staring at the ceiling, lost in his thoughts. I wish I could go to him and say the right words, but he needed time. I needed time.

My stomach growled. I walked to my living quarters and found Cassy had delivered a heaping plate of carry-out pizza, two cans of orange soda, and a chocolate-covered peanut butter bar. I groaned in anticipation of taking a bite of takeout food. It was difficult to bring food from the outside for fear the Ganders were near.

As I ate, I called for Ray in my mind. I needed his help, but he never answered. Mindlessly, I shoved food into my mouth and stared at the wall, my brain void of thought. I didn't hear anyone enter my dwelling until they spoke.

"Meadow, is it okay for us to come in?"

Shocked, I turned to see Beth and Dr. Ross standing in my doorway.

"Sure," I said wiping pizza sauce from my face. "Please come in, have a seat." I gestured to the empty chairs on either side of me.

"We have some alarming news."

The pizza crust I had been chewing on became a dry wad of cardboard in my mouth. I tried to swallow it, but the dry dough stuck in my throat. "What is it?"

Dr. Ross nodded and averted his eyes. He appeared at a loss for words. I looked at Beth. "You…have extremely low traces of transporter serum in your blood; it's almost nonexistent."

"How is that possible? I mean I have had that stuff running through my veins for years and suddenly poof…it's gone?" I asked. Several weeks ago, I would have done anything to be normal again, but now—it was a part of who I was.

"Right now, we don't know. But we believe with each visit to Hell you lost a bit of your transportability."

"Do you think that is why I started conforming into a fiend more quickly the last few times I transported?"

"It's definitely a possibility. We don't know right now," Dr. Ross replied.

"What do we do? If I can't go back, Evan will die."

"Have you been able to contact Ray?" Beth asked.

"No." I shook my head. The crunch of metal filled my ears. I looked down at my hands, shocked to see the can of soda I had drank moments before was crushed in my palms. "I've been trying to reach him, but I haven't heard anything. Do you think I can only communicate with him when I have the serum in my blood?"

Beth closed her eyes. "I don't know. He hasn't answered me either. We need to tell the others."

"What do we tell them?"

"The truth—and we need to bring the Jacobses in as well. They have a right to know."

"This will kill them." I hung my head, knowing once again I would be a disappointment to them.

"It will," Beth agreed. Her bluntness cut me to the core.

"Why can't you inject me again?"

"What?" Dr. Ross asked, a tiny glimmer of hope beamed in his eyes.

"Like with more transporter serum."

"We don't have any. Years ago your mother and father stole the only serum that was left." Dr. Ross deflated slightly.

"Yes, but didn't they find the empty case in my home? What if those tubes are still out there? What if my father has them?" Excitedly, I jumped to my feet, a plan formulating in my mind.

"We do believe your father has the serum, but we don't know where he is," Beth replied. "I'm afraid we don't have enough time to track him down *and* to save Evan."

Where would Dad hide? I have no idea…but maybe one of the Geeks would.

"Listen," I told the others, "we need to call an emergency meeting—like immediately. If we can find him, I will take another injection and I *will* save Evan. Have faith, guys. Evan is strong. You all are keeping watch over his body, right?"

Frustrated, Beth threw her hands in the air, and Dr. Ross nodded enthusiastically.

"This has nothing to do with faith. Even if we do find the serum in the next twenty-four hours or so—which is all the time Evan is likely to have left, what makes you think you can walk in, grab him, and go? You have been lucky so far, but the creatures of Hell will be on high alert looking for you. Plus, the Mezirot is gone, so you have no power or leverage."

Dr. Ross looked over at his wife. "She's right, Beth. We can't rely on science and logic right now. We must have faith!"

I smiled at Dr. Ross. He was right. God had protected all of us up to that point.

"Okay, we will call everyone to the dining hall then," Beth answered, defeated.

"Thanks, I will be there soon." I needed a few moments to mentally prepare my defense against the rest of the Geeks.

Chapter Thirty-Two

An Unwarranted Adventure

"You're crazy, you know that? Pure crazy! Your father is as deadly as a fiend," Cassy shrieked.

"Do you have a better plan?" I shot back.

"Since she has made up her mind, and to save precious time, I say let her go." Bubba chimed in at the risk of getting on Cassy's bad side. "However, you won't go alone. I will take you wherever you need to go."

"I don't care how you do it, but you *will* save our son," Evan's mother demanded. My head reeled, ready to bite back but one look at Mrs. Jacobs' red-rimmed eyes, and I softened. Mr. Jacobs, as usual, remained silent.

At the end of an hour filled with crying, demanding, and foot stomping, we had gotten nowhere, until Bubba offered his help. With his support, the rest of the Geeks conceded one by one.

Dr. Wright sat at a table by himself watching the confrontation but not offering any advice on what should be done. He looked troubled. While the Geeks grumbled amongst themselves about my best course of action, I made my way over to the doctor.

"Do you know where my father might be?" I asked.

He let out a huge sigh and looked me in my eyes. "There is only one place I can think of. When we were younger, your father and I enjoyed hunting. We went every weekend before they...um...acquired you. Then the trips kind of dwindled away. The cabin is in Waysville. It's a three-hour drive from here, but that is the only place I could think of where he would go."

"Does he have any family near?" I asked, hating to even ask. But considering recent revelations, I had to know.

Dr. Wright shook his head. "No, your father was adopted as well. By the time he turned twenty-one, his adoptive parents had both passed away, and he never found his real parents. When he and your mother met, all they wanted was to start a family and create a life they themselves never had, but Ray changed all of that for them."

As nice as it was to travel down memory lane, I didn't have time for it. "I'm going to need an address."

He dug in his pocket for a piece of paper and jotted something down. "Here."

I snatched the slip of paper from his outstretched fingers.

"There is an old gravel road past the drive that will take you the long way around. Pull about halfway up the drive—maybe half a mile—then walk the rest of the way so you can show up undetected."

"Everybody, listen up!" I shouted, jumping on top of the nearest table. "I have a lead and I'm taking Bubba with me. I need someone to keep a watch over Evan's body at all times from this point on. If he starts to crash, do what you have to do to save his life."

My eyes scanned the room and stopped on Cassy and Mrs. Romano. "Cass, I need you two to keep watch over Mark. He's not doing well. The rest of you keep up the normal operation of what is going on."

"Beth, continue to reach out to Ray," I said in my mind. Beth didn't react; I had lost my ability to communicate with her as well.

"Beth, can you try to reach Ray, please?" Beth gave me a curt nod.

Looking to my friend, I said, "Bubba, gather what you need, and I'll meet you back here in ten minutes. We need to get the serum and get back as soon as possible. Evan's life depends on it."

"Sure." Bubba strolled to Cassy and wrapped her in his arms. My heart ached with the desire to have someone care for me like that.

Taking the long way around, I hoped to catch a glimpse of Mark. He was awake. It was almost as if he sensed me coming and turned his head in my direction. Giving him a tight smile, I waved and kept walking as if on a mission. He didn't smile back but he waved me in.

Timidly, I stepped into his room. "Hi." I looked down at the floor.

"Hello," Mark said back, avoiding my eyes as much as I avoided his.

"You doing okay?" I asked.

He shrugged then nodded. I wished I hadn't come in; he seemed so distant.

"I'm going to find my dad." Those words got his attention. Mark's head shot up and he narrowed his eyes on me.

"He will kill you if he gets the chance." Mark's voice was void of emotion.

"I know," I whispered. "There is no more transporter serum in my blood. I have to get more, and my dad may have the last remaining vials of serum in existence."

Mark wrestled to sit up in his bed. "I have something to tell you. It's important."

The devastation on his face told me I didn't want to hear what he had to say.

"It will have to wait, I'm running behind already."

As I passed, I grazed his face lightly with my hand, knowing somehow things were going to be different between us, and then rushed out the door. Whatever Mark wanted to share was bound to bring me pain. I wasn't ready for more of that just yet.

"No, wait…" he called after me, but I pretended his words hadn't reached my ears and continued.

Chapter Thirty-Three

An Unlikely Turn

The trigger felt cool under his skin. His thumb twitched as he positioned the barrel under his jaw. Marcus squeezed his eyes shut, never seeing the rattler slither up from behind.

"Please, please, don't make me do this." Marcus sniffled through his tears.

A shocking pain radiated up his leg. The first strike was excruciating, but the serpent didn't stop there. It attacked again and again. Marcus dropped slowly to his knees, his upper body toppling over onto the dewy ground. Not finished with its onslaught, the snake sprung at Marcus' neck in a quick succession of three bites before it slithered away.

The rifle fell beside the boy's head, forgotten, as he lay on the ground feeling the poison flow through his veins.

He could've crawled home and gotten help, but it was better this way. Maybe his prayers were answered after all, and he wouldn't have to end his own life. Rolling to his back he looked up at the fading stars. It didn't take long before he lost consciousness. When his eyes closed for the last time, there was a brief period of darkness, then an intense white.

When his eyes opened once again, he had arrived at his final destination.

Chapter Thirty-Four

Departure

Bubba was still comforting Cassy when I re-entered the cafeteria. She was crying, begging him to talk sense into me.

"Cass, she has to do this, and you know it. If Evan dies without her trying, it will kill her." Bubba ran his hands over Cassy's silky hair.

"Trying to save him may kill her," Cassy said bitterly, jerking her head away from his hands.

Noticing my presence, she straightened her back and walked over to me. The anger in her eyes was replaced with the love she and I had shared since childhood. My heart softened as I realized how she, Bubba, and Evan had basically been forced to look out for me for all these years. The sting of their lost childhood shook me, but I would have done the same for them.

Cassy wrapped her arms around my neck and hugged me tight. "Be careful," she whispered.

I pulled back and looked into her eyes. "We will, I promise." I gave her another quick hug.

Mrs. Romano was still there but the rest of the Geeks had dispersed. "Take care of Cass for me," I said.

"Always," she answered, touching the side of my face with her hand. "Don't be afraid to do what you have to do, dear."

"Yes, ma'am," I answered.

I turned to Bubba. "Ready?"

"Yup, let's go."

We rode up the elevator in silence and exited the building. Cool night air greeted us. I wanted to stand there and bask in the moonlight. It felt like I had been underground for years instead of just weeks.

Bubba's old pickup truck was jacked up on tires that were taller than me. Anytime I rode with him, he had to boost me up into the cab. I couldn't help but laugh at the absurdity of having to be helped into the truck like a child.

Bubba climbed in on his side and started the truck. "You sure about this?" he asked.

"Yes," I replied, determinedly.

"Before we go, I would like to pray." Bubba twisted in his seat to face me.

I hesitated, not wanting to waste time but realizing how little time I had given God lately. "Yes, we have time for that."

"Good," Bubba said, grabbing my tiny hands in his massive ones. Bubba was a prayer warrior, and I was so glad he reminded me how important it was to talk with God—not only when times were good but amid hard times as well.

"Our almighty Father God, please be with Meadow and me as we embark on this journey to find the transporter serum. Father, we know this situation is dangerous, maybe even deadly, but we lift it into your hands, Father, and ask You to place a hedge of protection around us. Father, please be with Meadow. She has lost so much, and she is so special to so many of us. Please fill her with Your Spirit and give her strength in this last leg of her journey. Please allow our hearts to glorify and praise You through this storm. In Jesus' name we pray. Amen."

"Amen. Thank you." I was touched by Bubba's words. I felt a peace in knowing God was with us.

"You ready for this?" Bubba asked, his normal grin covering his face.

"Ready," I said back while clicking my seatbelt in place.

Bubba turned the engine over, spun the truck's tires, flinging gravel, and shot out into the night. I rolled down the window and let the wind blow through my hair, forgetting—at least for a little while—that I was on my way to an encounter that would most certainly end in a fight for my life.

THANK YOU

Thank you for reading The Cave of Darkness!

If you loved this book, please leave a review for me on Amazon.com and/or Goodreads.

Your reviews will help me in my craft and it makes my day to read a review from each and every one of you!

Please keep an eye on social media for book three, The Fire Cave, to be released later this year!

ABOUT THE AUTHOR

Rachel is a gal that wears many hats but her favorite is the Hogwarts sorting hat. She has already been sorted into Gryffindor, but she thinks best when adorned with the much loved headpiece. Rachel loves all things Harry Potter and chocolate. Rachel is an avid reader and loves to write in her free time. She is a Respiratory Therapist by day, and a children and youth director in her spare time. Rachel lives in Elizabethtown, KY with her husband and three beautiful daughters. Connect with Rachel below.

Website

Rachelrlopez.com

Social Media

Amazon.com/author/rachelrlopez
Facebook.com/rachelrenaylopez
Instagram.com/RachelRenaylopez
Twitter.com/rachel_r_lopez